*A Hogan for the Bluebird*

# A Hogan
## for the Bluebird

by ANN CROWELL

illustrated by HARRISON BEGAY

Charles Scribner's Sons    New York

*For Bill*

# Contents

# CHAPTER 1

# The Beauty Trail

HE WAKENED WHILE IT WAS STILL DARK AND, FROM HABIT, his first sleepy thoughts were of the horse.

It varied from time to time—this imaginary horse that carried him over the pastures. Sometimes it was black like his father's, then it would change to a sorrel or even a pinto like Johnny's. Once for a whole week it had been a pure white stallion.

There had been time enough for it to be every horse he had ever seen, for Little Eagle couldn't even remember when he hadn't wanted one of his own. He guessed he'd just been born wanting it. And the wanting had grown as he grew. Sometimes, now, it even got bigger than he, so big that his stomach would ache just from longing.

But not early mornings like this. This was the best time of all to think about the horse because then the wanting didn't hurt so much. While he waited for day to come, he could lie here and plan how he would train it and teach it to come at a whistle the way Johnny's horse did. He could think about all kinds of things they would do together, and the longing just stayed nice and gentle and sleepy—like a good friend, an old friend.

Today he meant, once and for all, to decide on the horse's name. But something kept bothering him—like a gnat that keeps getting in the way. Then the first dim mist of light crept under the blanket at the door and, suddenly, Little Eagle remembered.

He sprang up from his sheepskin and into his fine orange shirt. This was the day they were going for Sister! The trail of beauty to Singing Willow, to bring her back home from the mission boarding school. How could even sleepiness make him forget the day he had waited and waited for?

"You cross-eyed son of a she-pig," he muttered at the shirt's silver-dime buttons. They were giving him trouble again, but this was one time the shirt had to be fastened straight.

With the last dime finally buttoned, he slid quickly into his good buckskin pants and parted the blanket at the doorway.

Outside the hogan he stood lean and straight, his figure outlined against the mother-of-pearl white in the east. Then, as streaks of fire shot out from the rising sun, he made his morning prayer to Dawn Boy.

From a clump of yuccas came the sound of a turtle dove. A buzzard circled. The juniper scented the air. Behind his grandmother's loom a kid stood poised on the cantle of a saddle. Inside the hogan stirrings of life began, and in that time of dawn on the desert Little Eagle thought of the day ahead.

The family was ready long before Monty Blue Mountain came for them. Dressed in their finest, all waited in

a row outside the door—all but Many Rivers. The Old One did not approve of this school that had kept her granddaughter so long. She stood apart in handsome dignity, wrapped in her woolen blanket, her long gray hair bound into a knot with bright wool strips.

Laughing Rainbow, the boy's mother, wore a new calico skirt, and turquoise and coral adorned her velvet blouse. In her arms she held Little Echo, who played with her mother's bracelets. Little Eagle stood between his mother and father and glanced with pride at his father's purple shirt. Gray Wolf also wore the black sombrero the boy so admired.

At last, out of a cloud of dust, Monty Blue Mountain came—not with a team of horses nor in a truck *chidi* but a *real chidi*, the white man's kind where all could sit inside.

"Seven-Cylinders-One-Missing," Uncle Monty said with pride.

Sometimes Monty Blue Mountain worked on the tracks of the Iron Trail or at trucking sheep. But he liked best the work that took him trading, for then he went where there were lots of people. He liked busy places. He always wore levis and a hat like white cow herders, and he could rope as well as they and even talk their English.

Sitting beside Uncle Monty was Red-Bottle-Stand-Tall. Whenever he heard of anyone who was going to the mission, the tall one always went along to go in the hospital. For a little time the doctors would agree to let him stay while they studied him and tried to find the reason why he came. In a day or two they always turned him out and sent him home. But soon he was right there again. He liked the hospital.

What now? thought Little Eagle. Grandmother wouldn't get in! She never had been pleased with Uncle Monty's white-man ways. And this Seven-Cylinders-One-Missing had evil sounds and smells. She closed her arms across her breast and slowly shook her head.

The young boy's heart had almost stopped, but he waited with the rest while the Old One struggled with her thoughts. Not a single word was said. At such a time, when Sister was returning, surely she, the grandmother, would wish to go. They waited patiently.

Finally the Old One made up her mind to try Uncle's *chidi* and got in front. That was the very place he'd planned to ride! Of course by sitting there Grandmother wouldn't be near Father. A man must never look into the eyes of his wife's mother.

So Little Eagle heaved a sigh and climbed in beside his father. He wiggled every way he could to watch his uncle drive, but the tall one's head scarf blew in the way and Uncle was so wide.

Suddenly Grandmother said something to Uncle Monty that brought the *chidi* to a stop. No other word was spoken. She got out and reached in back to take his little baby sister, then loftily strode off toward home. It was Seven Cylinders Too Many!

Little Eagle nose-dived to the front to sit by Uncle Monty. Again the *chidi* started up and soon was moving swiftly. It bounced and banged along the trail. The boy was filled with pleasure, and when they passed his friend Johnny-Runs-Backwards with his sheep herd,

Little Eagle swelled with pride that almost burst his silver buttons. Even the sight of Johnny riding his own pinto pony didn't make Little Eagle feel this time that usual ache of wanting.

Lavender verbena, growing in riotous tangles, dotted the desert wastes, and wild tulips blew their petals like gold on the wind. Near a distant hogan, corn showed above the ground, for it was the season of tiny and tall leaves. And on the travelers flew, sailing over the sandy trail and bouncing over the ruts.

The sun was touching the distant cliffs by the time the talking wires appeared. Uncle Monty pointed out the place where Sam Red-Eye had borrowed a piece to mend his wagon. It had made the wires stop talking, but that had happened long ago. The talking wires had all been fixed by now.

Ahead of them a mirage danced with craggy buttes. Then the sand that blew in their faces grew pleasantly cool. A sharp, clean smell of sagebrush and cedar came on the desert air.

"Goin' to rain," said Monty Blue Mountain, and he pumped his foot to help the tired *chidi* along.

Sun Bearer started to paint the clay bluffs but quickly changed his mind. Pools of violet that shadowed the cliffs seeped farther into the sky. Now came the sound of thunder, soon black clouds were shutting out the light.

They had almost reached the turn-off when the rain came suddenly. Right then the *chidi* gave a gasp and rolled to a dead stop. While the rain came in upon them by the side that had no window and blew out through the other side that had a broken window, the family waited in the car with long and sober faces.

Then lightning shot out from the sky and lit up all below and they saw a covered wagon coming slowly from the right. Uncle Monty and Gray Wolf got out, braving the storm. They reached the turn-off just in time to flag the wagon down.

# CHAPTER II

# Lightning Strikes Twice

THE RAIN HAD STOPPED AND NIGHT WAS LONG UPON THEM by the time the wagon reached the mission gates, for the storm had made the road so badly rutted that the men had to help the mules over most of the way.

It was too late to visit Elder Sister. All the lights were out except those in the hospital. But inside that hogan there was much confusion, for lightning had struck a tree right outside its wall. If lightning strikes a tree inside the forest, The People consider it an accident, though they'll never go up close enough to touch it. But when it strikes near a house, that is very bad. It means that ghosts or witches are attacking, and maybe even Holy People, too. For though the Holy Ones had made Earth People, they also sometimes did unfriendly things. This was the second time that lightning's arrows had struck the pine tree by the hospital.

Little Eagle and his father stood with the rest at the window and watched the sick ones inside preparing to leave. Nurses, hurrying in and out in excitement, were trying to make everyone go back to bed.

A man rushed out, his belongings tied in a blanket slung over his back. And after him came a white man calling angrily. The second man was the doctor, Red-Bottle-Stand-Tall said, and he wanted the first man to go back in. He was telling him that Dan Chee had already gone for the medicine man. Dan Chee now followed Jesus and worked at the mission church. But he was Navajo and understood this fear in his people.

Suddenly a voice boomed forth and it seemed to be everywhere. Little Eagle jumped in terror, for he thought witches must be closing in all around.

But Red-Bottle-Stand-Tall knew about hospitals. He explained the box that the doctors used to send their messages. And while the boy was still marveling about the magic box, there came another voice, speaking Navajo. It was *Hatali,* their tribal medicine man.

The sheepherder tingled clear down to his toes as the ceremony for routing evil began. Through the talking box the singing chant reached into every room, and across the campus to all the cabins and halls. It seemed to be the voice of Great Sky Father.

Then when the chant was ended Little Eagle saw him. Through the windows he saw *Hatali* go into the rooms. With his feathered prayer stick and four snakes made from trees struck by lightning, he made a prayer over each of those who were sick. Then he sprinkled them with medicine from his basket. Some of the people paid for his blessing with turquoise. Little Eagle was astounded at the power of this Holy Way Priest.

After he had cleansed the evil spirits from within, the medicine man came out of the hospital and went over to the burned pine tree. There was not a sound from the gathering that made way for him to pass. And as he dipped the feathered wand again in the buckskin pouch and flung the medicine drops onto the tree, the whole desert seemed to throb with *Hatali's* chant.

By the time the ceremonial came to an end, all was again *hozoni*. Now the sick people were once more on the path of blessing from the gods, for the harmony way was restored both within and without. Inside the hospital they left off talk of leaving and returned to their beds.

That night, for the first time in his life, Little Eagle also slept in a bed. But he was the only one who did, except for Red-Bottle-Stand-Tall. The others spread their blankets and lay on the floor.

Navajos who have always slept on the ground don't find beds comfortable. The cots in the visitor's hall were seldom used. But to Little Eagle the lively bedsprings were a wonder and delight. He romped in flips and headstands long after the rest were asleep. By the time his moccasined feet were too tired for any more bouncing, all that could be heard were the snores from Red-Bottle-Stand-Tall.

Lying there in the dark and quiet, Little Eagle saw the moon rise. He watched it through the hole cut in the wall. The hole was covered with the magic stone that one could see through. "Weendow" Uncle Monty said was the name.

Ei-yie! What a trail of beauty this day had been! But before he could finish a sigh, sleep had carried Little Eagle back to his sheep on the mesa. Once again he was a tiny boy walking with tall Sister and clinging to her billowing skirt as she followed the flock. She was telling him all the things he must learn about herding, the smell of the seasons and where the good pastures lie. He

shivered and clung closer still as she told of the witches, for now the night was closing in all around.

Suddenly Singing Willow was no longer with him. She had gone far away and left him to tend the sheep, so he spread down his blanket and lay there under the sky roof and watched the sky "weendows" as, one by one, stars peeked through. But time dragged and dragged as he waited for Singing Willow, so he counted the stars—one by one—by one—by—one . . .

*CHAPTER III*

# The Return

THE COMMENCEMENT EXERCISES WERE BEING HELD IN A large hall, but the family of Gray Wolf had seats on the very front row. From up on the stage where the graduates sat in rows facing the crowd, Singing Willow looked down on them once and smiled shyly.

"She sits in beauty," thought Little Eagle, his heart swelling with pride. "She's going back with us. She's coming home!" The words sang in his mind like a chant. Once more his sister's song would carry over the mesa as she sat with the metate for grinding corn. Each day would be like sunlight now and the Old One again content.

To the sheepherder it seemed that the speaker giving the address would never run out of breath. But finally he did, and then Dan Chee told in Navajo what he had said. It was a funny story about one called Mohammed, who told a mountain to walk right over to him. But the mountain wouldn't obey, so Mohammed went to the mountain. Then Dan Chee said Singing Willow and the rest must now go meet their mountains. It was strange advice to the boy who tended sheep.

When Dan Chee sat down, the white man rose again and read the names of all those sitting with Singing

Willow, and, one by one, each received from him a rolled paper tied with ribbon. His sister's name was the last, but when the man said it he called her "Irene." That was the name the school had given her.

After Singing Willow received her gift, she walked over and sat at a chest with big black and white teeth. Whatever was his sister going to do? Then softly and gently there came sounds like rippling water.

Little Eagle's mouth fell open. His sister was making these sounds by putting her hands on the strange-looking teeth. He looked toward his mother but quickly back, for now his sister's fingers were flying over the teeth and the rippling water had changed to a rising wind.

Before his eyes there came a vision of the Holy People standing in a circle around a buckskin on the ground. Under it were two ears of corn, white and yellow, with their tips toward the east. All waited for Niltsi the Wind to breathe upon the buckskin and make the corn man and woman. Three times Hasyelti, the Dawn god, peeked under the buckskin, then smoked his pipe and blew smoke rings to the sky. But the fourth time Hasyelti saw with joy that the white ear of corn had turned into a man and the yellow into a woman. Niltsi had entered their heads and come out through their toes and fingers. Grandmother said that was why toes and fingers have little circled ridges where the wind whirled through when Niltsi gave the breath of life. Many times Little Eagle had heard the story of how man and woman were made. And now, by his sister's magic, he had even seen it.

Later on, Singing Willow took her family over the

mission grounds and at dark a bonfire was built for the feasting and games.

But Monty Blue Mountain had disappeared after Singing Willow's ceremonial and didn't come back to the sleeping hogan all night, so early the following morning Gray Wolf decided to leave and gathered his family together to go home on foot.

They left Red-Bottle-Stand-Tall feigning pain in his little finger, for one must have a hurt to go in hospital. But after the hospital people painted red on the place he'd scratched, they told Red-Bottle-Stand-Tall to go on home. "Tell him this isn't a hotel," they said to Singing Willow. And the girl repeated their words in Navajo. But the tall one only increased his groans and settled down on the floor, so the family of Gray Wolf started on their way.

Little Eagle didn't mind leaving the tall one—he was making such frightful sounds and rolling his eyes almost to the top of his head—but he did wish they would wait for Monty Blue Mountain. He felt sure his uncle had gone to get help for Seven-Cylinders-One-Missing. Maybe, since it had had a nice rest, the *chidi* would go again.

But his sister, too, was eager to be leaving, for she was filled with joy at going home. Yet, as they were walking out through the gates of the mission, Little Eagle saw her turn back and look over the grounds—at the church and the schoolrooms and play yards and many fine buildings, the hall where they ate and the one of the music sounds. Her eyes seemed to linger now on the homes for the teachers and those for the students, on the one where she'd lived so long. For a fleeting moment he thought her lower lip trembled, but she quickly turned and ran on to catch up with the rest.

It was nice and cool for walking; the sun not yet risen. Then before they reached where the sky touched the grove of cedars, a truckload of sheep came along and pulled to a stop. In the truck was the trading-post man, who was going their way, as far as their turn-off. They might as well ride, he said.

There was not room enough for everyone in the front part, so the boy and his sister sat in back with the sheep. But now Singing Willow didn't seem to like sheep near her. She made faces and held her nose until she got out.

At the place where their trail turned off from the road, the *chidi* waited still. But Monty Blue Mountain was nowhere about, so the family continued on their way with Gray Wolf leading, followed by Laughing Rainbow. Singing Willow fell in along beside Little Eagle, and he saw with surprise that his height almost equalled hers. When he was little he stood way down below her, but now the top of his head came up to her brow. .

"You have grown since I've been away, my brother," she told him. Had she heard his thoughts? "You've almost caught up with me now." Her admiring smile so filled him with pleasant confusion that he couldn't seem to lift his eyes from the ground.

As they trudged along, the family chewed on jerky and at noon stopped under the shade of a juniper tree. While they rested, Singing Willow undid the carton she carried and handed each a colored lollipop. These were a "good-by" present from one of her teachers—the one who had taught her to make the music sounds.

Little Eagle was still in awe of his sister because of those music sounds. But now with happiness bright on her face as she talked, he ventured questions. And in no time at all he learned many things. The ceremonial was "commencement" in the white man's tongue, and the big chest with teeth was called "piano." But the black and white teeth weren't teeth at all; the name of them was "keys."

Singing Willow told this and other things, too, and the telling filled her with gladness. Little Eagle hung on her every word and yearned to hear still more. Then he saw that his mother and father would not even listen. They had closed their ears to their daughter's talk, and he easily guessed the reason—these things that filled Singing Willow's head were not of her own people. His mother and father just stared straight ahead, silently lapping their lollipops. In the juniper tree a mourning dove made his sad sound.

The way grew longer and longer and the sun blazed down like fire. Yet a dark cloud seemed to follow overhead. For since the lollipops his sister walked in pensive silence, and she also walked as though her foot were hurt. He reached out and took the carton to relieve her of its load. Yet this didn't seem to lighten her strange gloom.

Things were all mixed up. Their going home should be a time of gladness. Everything was beautiful the day they came. And they were going back by the way that they had come. Yet, going home now, nothing looked the same.

Much later Gray Wolf led them across Red Top Mesa to shorten the way. But even with the short cut they could not reach home this day. He hoped when the shadows lengthened from the buttes that his father would find a place for them to sleep. He longed for night to come, bringing its coolness. The hot sun made him miserable with thirst. He would gladly have traded his jackknife for some water. But the water they'd brought along was now all gone.

They came to the brush corral of a camp where a flock grazed peacefully, the herder sound asleep on his quiet horse. Some sheep were at the water hole and Little Eagle, too, bent to drink while his sister took some moccasins from her carton. And as she removed the stiff school shoes and put on those Gray Wolf had made, the look in her father's eyes began to change. Instead of blankness now they held his look of home and family.

Little Eagle breathed a sigh of relief. Soon he was thinking once again of the horse for which he yearned. The sight of that sleeping horse and man had made the longing return. "Some day," his father always said. "I'll buy you a horse some day." But when could that day ever come? They never had much money. All he'd ever had of his own were just the dimes on his shirt and some pennies. Even with the dimes and his knife and arrows and bow—and his shirt as well—there wouldn't be enough to start a trading post "owe-you" deal.

As he walked along, Little Eagle's face was puckered in deep thought. Suddenly, it lit up with an inspiration. The lambing had been good this spring; his own sheep had increased. Maybe he could sell his share to buy the horse. Of course they really weren't just his, those with his private earmark. Each sheep was earmarked to some family member, but all the family owned the flock. No part was ever traded or sold without their whole consent. They must be in agreement.

He liked to think, and he often did, of this family plan of The People—how the old and the children looked after the sheep while the men tended horses and cattle. Men built fences, too, and all the corrals; hauled water and wood and did plowing. They dressed the skins and made moccasins. Some were silversmiths like his father.

The women looked after the children and cooked and kept the hogan in order. They butchered the mutton and gathered the crops. Sometimes they made pots and baskets. In their spare time, of course, they sat to weave. The men always built the hogans, but sometimes the women did the chinking. Sometimes they even helped plaster, as his mother and grandmother did that time they built Grandmother a new one. They had to build a new hogan for her since Grandfather "went away" inside the old one.

Suddenly, Little Eagle laughed, for he hadn't even noticed they were back again on their former trail. He'd been too busy thinking. Singing Willow's foot no longer hurt, and now she walked with her mother. From up by his father's side, where he walked, he could hear them laughing together.

Then from out of the blaze of sun at their backs came a chugging and chortling sound. The boy gave a war whoop and leaped in the air, and the rest broke into broad smiles.

With a cloud of dust and a screeching of sound, the *chidi* pulled to a stop. "Got it fixed," said Monty Blue

Mountain. But that was all. Though Uncle spoke two tongues, he never wasted words with either.

So the family climbed in and Uncle Monty passed out the pop he had brought. Then Seven-Cylinders-One-Missing started up and again they were on their way. The *chidi* now frisked and romped along to make up for lost time. The final miles went sailing swiftly by. Even before darkness had settled over the land, the car brought the family to the end of the trail. With a loud cough of victory, then, the *chidi* stopped.

Last streaks of red were dying in the sky and a tantalizing aroma came on the air, for the Old One had made the cookfire outside tonight in honor of her granddaughter's homecoming. She stood there with head held high, her hair blowing in the breeze. As they approached, a quiet came over all, for this was the longed-for moment of return.

At first the young girl's steps were shy and hesitant; then in a run she reached the Old One's side. Strongly they clasped their hands, each in the other's, and with a graceful gesture of symbolic caress, the Old One's blanket swept out to enfold the young girl. This is my child, it meant. I would shield her still, from the harsh winds that blow ever on the earth. And the young head went down on the Old One's shoulder. This is my mother's mother, dear and beloved. I reverence her, it meant.

Little Eagle's eyes burned. The trail had finished in beauty after all. But better than anything else right then was that excellent smell of goat stew from the cookpot fire.

# CHAPTER IV

# The Door of Jenny Chee

LITTLE ECHO HAD TAKEN HER FIRST STEPS WHILE THE family was away, and one week later she was toddling everywhere on her fat little legs.

"Now that she knows what they're for, she won't let them rest," said Laughing Rainbow, smiling down at the baby who followed her about, holding onto a handful of her skirt.

"She walks like Torn Shirt does when he has had too much fire water," said Little Eagle. He sat by the cookpot, munching on a handful of liver. "Come, Torn Shirt, and leave your mother in peace." He reached out and pulled his baby sister down on his lap. "Sit awhile or you will wear out your legs before our father has finished making your moccasins."

His words made his mother laugh as she stooped to remove the empty food bowls from the sheepskin spread on the ground, wool side down. And at Little Echo's aping of her mother's sounds, all broke into laughter—all but Gray Wolf.

"Mine are women of many noises," he said, pretending sternness he did not feel. "One sings, one laughs and the other echos both." He arose and gave a gentle tug to the Little One's hair before passing through the hogan door to the outside.

"She will no longer have need of this," said Singing Willow, picking up the cradle board, "and it is just as well. A cradle board makes a baby's head flat in the back."

Little Eagle and his mother examined the back of Little Echo's head while Singing Willow put the cradle board away. No one had noticed the grandmother's tall figure now standing in the doorway.

Having stowed the cradle board in a low corner of the rafters, the girl turned around in time to see her brother holding his tin cup for the Little One to drink. "Don't do that," she said to him.

"But she is thirsty!" The boy was too astonished to hold onto the cup which Singing Willow took from his hand. Little Echo let out a howl of disappointment.

"Coffee is bad for children," Singing Willow said, "but the Little One is too young to know. I will get some milk for her." She picked up a pottery bowl and started toward the outside.

At the door Many Rivers stood aside to let her grand-daughter pass, then came on into the room. She and Laughing Rainbow exchanged looks silently. The mother raised her shoulders and let them fall, then turned to finish stacking the pots by the fire under the smokehole in the center roof.

The Old One poured some coffee into an empty tomato tin and settled down to drink. "The white man's taint—it lingers over long," she said.

Laughing Rainbow rolled up the sheepskin before

she answered. "It is only five suns." She put the spoons in the box nailed to the wall by the door which served as a cupboard for their supplies. Then she, too, poured coffee from the pot and settled down to drink. For a time the women sipped their coffee in silence. Little Echo was also quiet now, happy again with the liver her brother had given her.

The silence had grown heavy when Laughing Rainbow spoke. "Soon we shall need to make the trail for more salt." Navajos made long journeys to get salt from the sacred salt deposits. It could be ground as fine as one wished and was not so bitter to the taste as salt sold at the trading post.

But Many Rivers would not speak of salt. Something more urgent was on her mind. Again came that puzzling silence which troubled the boy. It was not like the silence he knew while tending his sheep—the stillness of mesas that broke into shadowed cliffs, that spoke to him from towering red canyon walls. That was a quiet he understood and loved—like the wistful silence of a willow tree growing alone or the shouting silence of mountain peaks sun-topped with red. The silence of such things was beautiful, it was *nezhoni*, but this new silence of the women made too much noise. It seemed the trickster coyote made sport these days. One minute, inside the hogan all was *hozoni*. Then like a day that cannot make up its mind, the clouds rolled in, shutting out the harmony way.

Little Eagle ached for the sound of his mother's laugh, but no laughter came with her words "It will go away"—just a sigh.

*30*

"It lingers over long," the Old One repeated. And this time Little Eagle read the meaning in her words. His sister still held to the strangeness of white men's ways. Like yesterday when Little Echo had held the green apple, Singing Willow had said, "It will make her stomach hurt." But Navajo children always had eaten green apples—and drunk coffee from the time they could drink from a cup. Little Echo had been so content just holding the apple, for it was really too hard for her young teeth to bite. But it seemed Elder Sister was always taking joy from the small one. And her taking milk from the goat in these little amounts, surely that was not good. It would make the goat go dry, and her milk was necessary for the young kid. How strange that his sister's return, which brought happiness, had also brought with it these things that darkened the peace.

"I shall ask her father to go for the medicine man," said his mother. "When tomorrow's sun rests, we will have the Blessing Way."

Her words were what his grandmother had wanted to hear. "It is well," she said.

He rose to leave.

Waiting for the last of the sheep to file out of the pen, Little Eagle watched his sister return with the milk to the hogan. How pretty she looked once more in her Navajo dress. With her homecoming the school clothes had been stored away, along with the family's fine clothing and hard jewelry goods. Before Singing Willow had even gone into the hogan, Grandmother had sprinkled the cornmeal and pollen on her. Yet his sister was still not free of the white man's taint. Well, *Hatali* was coming to sing the Blessing Way, and that ceremony always brought harmony. Yes, peace would soon be restored in their home once again.

Knowing this, the boy shook off his troubled thoughts like the drops of water a dog shakes off his skin. In dismay, he found he had completely forgotten to sing the sheep song that he always sang while the flock was passing out of the gray-poled corral. It must be that his head was not tight on his shoulders. Today, the right way of doing things seemed tossed by the wind.

"Come, Taggo," he called, then saw that his words were not needed. Already the dog was trotting ahead with the sheep. They went past the kettle of dye near the storage dugout; past the squash bed, its leaves shining brightly green in the sun; then around the cool-house that sheltered them in hot summer with its oak-leaf roof that rustled and stirred in the breeze.

At the top of the mesa he turned around to look again at his home. Singing Willow was running toward him. She ran like a deer.

"You forgot your food," she called, and waved the buckskin pouch at him. He waited until she reached his side. She was laughing and all out of breath. "You would be very hungry before you return." She handed him the pouch, then said, "I will walk with you for a while, it is such a pleasant day."

Again Little Eagle felt that pleasure that kept his eyes on the ground, so they walked without speaking until Singing Willow began to hum a tune. It was the one she had played that day at school on the piano.

"What is that you sing?"

"Do you think it good? It's one I made myself. I call it 'My Bluebird Dream,'" she said, then bent to pull up a root. It was a canaigre root. When boiled, it made dye of a yellow brown. "This kind our grandmother needs for the rug. I will take it back to her."

Singing Willow's turquoise and white shell beads did a dance as she tugged and pulled. But the root was holding fast to the soil, so Little Eagle bent to help. Then suddenly it came free and both tumbled backwards onto the ground.

Laughing, they picked themselves up and now the talking came easier as they walked to the canyon's rim and gazed at that ancient place below, which was cut right out of the side of the cliff. It seemed to hang on the very edge—the dwelling of First People.

On the canyon's floor they could even see the greenness of growing things. And here and there the hogan homes of their kin and clan relatives.

Singing Willow shaded her eyes and said, "I see our cousin's peach trees. I can almost see their blossoms. If I had binoculars, I know I could." Then she told him about binoculars that one looked through to see. They were like two round eyes made of glass that brought far-off things near. His sister knew no end of wonders that he liked to hear.

He had never cared for all that talk about his going to school when those white ones came and said he ought to go. He was glad he couldn't go, that he was needed for the sheep. Still, he would like to see through those two round magic eyes. And now with Sister home to tend the flock, they would expect him.

"How is it at that school?" he asked. "Did everything seem strange?"

"At first it did."

"When Johnny went he only stayed two days."

"That happens," Singing Willow said. "Sometimes they run away."

"Why didn't you?"

"I never thought of it, I guess. I was too sick with longing. I wanted so to be back home I cried and cried for days. But one day I was cleaning up the room with the piano, and when I dusted off the keys they made the music sounds. I found that touching different ones could make them tell a story. I didn't know someone was listening. After that, they let the music teacher show me how to play. And finally the sickness went away."

"But did you never wish again to be back with The People?"

"Oh, many times. I always thought about my home and family. But the sickness never came back after I had learned to play."

The stone of the canyon was carved out in many hues and colors. For a time they stood and looked at all the reds and whites and orange. Then they turned away from the canyon's rim and took a sloping trail.

The sky was like a painting made of purest, clearest blues, and the heavy rain had brought out desert flowers of many shades.

They came upon a little knoll that overlooked a hogan almost hidden by sagebrush and weeds, for it was now deserted. They had started toward it when Little Eagle stopped in sudden fear.

"*Chindi! Chindi!*" he cried. "That hogan is *chindi!*"
Quickly he grabbed his sister's arm and turned to run
away, for he'd seen the hogan was partly burned, which
meant it was a place where ghosts and witches often
came to work their evil spells.

He was pulling her so fast Singing Willow panted as
she said, "It was where one called Long Ears died. I
even saw the hole."

He knew a hole would be in the wall but hadn't
waited to see, for a burned hogan also meant that someone had "gone away" while inside. But what had made
his sister say that old Long Ears had died? The animals
indeed did die; people just "went away." Perhaps
Singing Willow had learned so much while at the boarding school that she no longer remembered things she
knew so well before.

He slowed down now. They were far enough away
from the *chindi* place. But Singing Willow's talk still
lingered on that one departed. "Old Long Ears' wife has
since become the wife of Blue Chips' brother."

He smiled. His sister's woman talk was so much like
their mother's.

They headed toward a valley bright with dodgeweed
all in bloom. The aspen and oak and pine looked dark
on the far-off mountainsides. Yet the sheepherder knew
if he were near they would be all kinds of green. How
much he would like to bring them close with those two
round magic eyes.

But Singing Willow's thoughts were still on Blue
Chips' brother's wife. "At the hogan which she lives in
now, there is a wooden door."

He wished his sister would forget her idle woman

chatter long enough to let her eyes behold the buttes that danced with colors. Before she'd gone away, when they had walked out on the mesa they had looked for rainbows and watched the mountain shadows shape like monsters; she had told about the heroes, named the sheep and all their children.

Now she said, "The hogan of one Jenny Chee, my friend at school—her hogan, too, has a door of wood, even a wooden floor."

He knew about his sister's friend whose name was Jenny Chee. She was the daughter of Dan Chee, the Navajo at the mission. This Jenny also had received a paper tied with ribbon. But with all her wooden door and floor, she couldn't make the music.

Still, Singing Willow kept on talking of that door of Jenny's. "It both opens and it shuts," she said, with something like a sadness.

Her steps grew slow. She lagged behind, so he turned back to see. She had stopped. And now she let the root slide right out of her hand. Suddenly, without a word, she turned and went back home.

He kicked a rock. Of all the empty-headed, silly sisters! She'd left him like she dropped the root—as though not worth the bother. He had waited for this time, to be with her back on the pasture. But she hadn't, she no longer cared—for him, or sheep, or mesa.

He kicked the rock another time in angry, bitter hurt, then sniffed and swiped his sleeve across his eyes and then his nose. Not for Sister would he ever shed a tear. What did she matter! It was only that he'd hurt his toe on that stupid old rock.

But it seemed that somewhere now he heard the sly trickster coyote, laughing like he always did whenever people lost *hozoni.*

# CHAPTER V

# Strange Music on the Wind

THE FAMILY HAD TO WAIT FOR THE BLESSING WAY. The medicine man was making a ten-day Sing. While they waited, Gray Wolf and Laughing Rainbow took part of the flock to the vats for dipping sheep.

The *chidi* which had taken them in splendor to see the elder sister graduate had finally settled down to rest forever. But Uncle, who again was in the business of hauling stock, came for them in his truck.

This time Little Echo made the journey, sitting happily on Laughing Rainbow's lap up in front beside her uncle and her father. Her brother and her sister didn't go. Little Eagle's help was needed with the shearing, and Singing Willow said she'd stay at home rather than ride in back with all those sheep.

The grandmother had started on the shearing while the family had been visiting at school, so they took this fleece along to sell or trade it. The trading post was near the government vats.

For a time it was a happy little circle that worked at shearing by the storage place. Uncle Monty's older wife had come to help them, and now she tied the sheep and held them still while Little Eagle and the Old One clipped them. Singing Willow sorted out and stacked the wool.

When the young girl stopped to work awhile at carding, her brother said, "Why do you card it now? The dirt will help it weigh more for the selling."

But his sister said, "I do not card to sell. This that I comb and clean is for Grandmother to dye for use in weaving the rug." And as she combed the dirt out of the clippings, Singing Willow sang a happy little song.

But after a time the young girl's singing became a lonesome hum. Then she laid aside her work to walk about. She inspected the growing beans and squash and pulled a few weeds from the ground. The boy saw she no longer was *hozoni*.

Later, Singing Willow went into the hogan and brought out the bedding to air. She placed the sheepskins and blankets over the pole between two trees, then returned for her skirts and her mother's, which she also hung out to air. Now she seemed at a loss for something else to do.

Turquoise Horse moved among the pillars of the sky, his hoofs shod with silver, his mane strung with white shell beads. Yet the girl did not seem to notice the fair summer day. She stood with a far-off look in her eyes. Was she thinking again of that door? Little Eagle wondered.

The grandmother and his uncle's wife didn't notice, so busy were they with their talking and the work. Little Eagle wished his uncle had brought the other wife. The younger wife seemed always to bring Sister cheer since her years were closer to those of Singing Willow. The older aunt was nearer to Grandmother's years.

Now Singing Willow had wandered out of sight. Perhaps she was grinding corn on the metate. Soon Little Eagle was lost in his same old dream. As he clipped the sheep he thought of the horse he so longed for and the way he would train it and which would be best of the names. He had hoped for the horse before the time of Cold Woman, but it wouldn't be wise to speak of selling now. The Blessing Way would cost them both sheep and money, so he might as well forget his selling plan. With a sigh he brought his thoughts back to the shearing.

Singing Willow could not be grinding corn after all. If she were, he would hear the grating sound of the two stones. Perhaps she had gone to take another walk. She often went walking these days—but always without him. Not that he cared. It made no difference to him.

A sheep escaped and trotted into the hogan, but they didn't bother to get it; the sheep would return. Were his sister inside it would shoot out like an arrow. Singing Willow didn't like the sheep to go into the house. Whenever one wandered in she scared it silly and used the batten or grass broom to drive it out.

The women had made the cookfire outside today, and now the beans were done and the bubble bread brown, so they ate and listened to Uncle's wife tell a story. It was a funny one she had heard her own grandmother tell. While The People had been imprisoned at Fort Sumner, the Blue Coats had given to them the coffee beans. The People did not know about coffee, so they had cooked the beans. For four days they cooked them, but never were they fit to eat. "But they learned to like the water they boiled them in." Uncle Monty's wife laughed and showed where her front teeth were missing. Little Eagle wished Singing Willow had been there to hear.

The old ones seemed in no haste to return to the shearing, so the boy decided to take a walk for awhile. It wasn't that he meant to seek out Singing Willow, he told himself. He just felt like moving about and looking around.

Old Taggo, asleep in the shade at the side of the hogan, woke up long enough to see what his master would do. "No work today," he was told. "Go on with your sleeping." Little Eagle laughed then, for he saw that his words were not needed. Sleep had already caught the dog once again in its web.

He had wandered far before he heard sounds of music. They came like the singing of wind as it gently rose. But, no—they were like the sounds of his sister's piano, the music she'd made that day with the magic keys. And yet, not quite. It was more like his sister's singing. But that could not be. It came from across the wash. Singing Willow would never go close to Grandmother's old hogan. Like Long Ears, Grandfather too had "gone away" while inside. No one went near such places for fear of ghost sickness, the evil let loose by Woman Speaker when she died. She sent it because First Boy and First Girl who buried her had not put her left moccasin on her right foot. Nor the right one on her left foot, as they should have done. Grandmother told of it as they sat round the hogan fire on cold winter nights.

The rising of wind could often make sounds like music. No, it had not been Singing Willow—just singing wind. The boy turned to look about and saw old Taggo, a small speck black and white, loping over the waste.

He waited until the dog was there beside him. "So you conquered your laziness after all," he said.

Taggo wagged his tail in answer, then followed his master, and soon Little Eagle returned for the shearing again.

His sister still had not returned when he reached the hogan. By the time she came, the sun was atop the tall rocks. But she came home singing and laughing. She was happy again. To Little Eagle she was, indeed, a puzzle. One moment the lights of spring would dance in her eyes, but then they would cloud over with a dullness, as though she saw cold winter's sullen skies.

The long day's work had finally been completed when a piece of yellow moon came into view. It rose as the sun went down, painting a picture of splendid fire to welcome in the night. With this final splash of brilliance in the heavens the weary travelers reached home. In the truck were Uncle, Mother and Little Echo—the baby sound asleep in her mother's arms. But the sheep that had gone to the dip were not there with them. In the back of Uncle's truck were only a few. And where was Father? Then Little Eagle saw him. Gray Wolf came on a horse quite far behind.

The horse, an Indian pony, was a mare of great beauty. The gold of her coat was as pale as lightest corn. But her mane was black and her hoofs had long black feathers. Gray Wolf had her in a walk, for both were tired. Still the mare stepped gracefully, with a gentle fineness.

Suddenly Little Eagle's heart was pounding wildly.

For his father dismounted and came toward him with the mare, and he saw that her forehead bore that wonderful marking, the black star—four-pointed, like the fire in the House of the Stars, the one centered on sand paintings for Big Star Chant. Never had he seen a buckskin with such a marking. Surely there had not been a horse like this before.

He could not speak, he was so struck with her beauty. Nor hear, for the hope that pounded loud at his heart.

But he heard when his father said, "You have long been patient. Now care for this mare, my son. She belongs to you."

The boy gazed up at the mare like one enchanted, as Gray Wolf placed the pony's rein in his hand. Then he took a single slow step to approach his treasure, but stopped and cast his eyes back to the ground. Such confusion of awe and joy and wonder had seized him that he couldn't seem to lift his head again.

The mare eyed the small, still figure there before her, then stretched out her neck to nuzzle the downcast head. With that came release of Little Eagle's love and longing, and his arms shot up to encircle the animal's neck. Happiness tears sprang hot to his eyes. The earth was spinning. He buried his face in the mane of his own Black Star.

# CHAPTER VI

# Two Friends

THE PLAN FOR THE BLESSING WAY WAS COMPLETELY FOR-
gotten. There was no longer a need for that expense.
Black Star not only brought happiness to Little Eagle
but to everyone in the family. Singing Willow's delight
that he had his longed-for pony was almost as great as
the boy's own joy in the mare. Now her effort to change
their Navajo manner of living was quite forgotten, and
also her "white people" talk. And she no longer went
off alone, causing them to worry. They could always
tell where she was by the sound of her song.

Laughing Rainbow's rippling laughter was almost
constant. *Hozoni* floated about like thistle down. Little
Echo squealed blissfully most of the day without reason,
since she couldn't have understood what was going on.
Gray Wolf shook his head as though in despair of his
women, but ended up grinning at all their happy noise.

There was only one time when the harmony hung in
a balance. It happened that very next day after Black
Star had come. Little Eagle had risen early to build her
a shelter and was busy with tree limbs and boughs,
making her a stall, when Singing Willow awakened and
came to join him.

"I can help," she said, "and we'll get it more quickly done."

"If you want to help, you can bring me a bucket of water. When I finish with this I'm going to wet her down."

"It would be in the way while we work. We might tip it over."

Till now Little Eagle hadn't even turned around. "Where did you get those?" he exclaimed.

"Get what?"

"Those levis?"

"From my box of school clothes. I climbed up and got them down."

"Pants! For school?"

"Not to classes. But always when hiking or riding. Or for games and sports and other such things," she said.

"Pants on women!"

"They're levis."

"I have eyes," he told her sharply, "but why should you wear them?"

"Because they're better than skirts for climbing around." Singing Willow's pretty eyes were suddenly brimming with laughter.

"Well, our grandmother wouldn't find pleasure in seeing you so."

Her laughter came bubbling then, like a cadence of music. "But everyone wears them, my brother, she surely knows."

Little Eagle gave a shrug and turned back again to his sawing. Singing Willow set about making braids of Black Star's mane and tail.

When the mare's stall was finished, they brought in

her feed and water, then together they worked to groom her and make her shine. Little Eagle sponged her coat with some of the precious water, and Singing Willow even used yucca suds for washing her star.

They were chattering gaily and so occupied with the grooming neither was aware that the Old One had approached—till her words bit the air with the grimness of her displeasure.

"And how, then, am I to tell which one is the son?"

They looked at each other. Then slowly they turned to face her, and it seemed to the boy she was suddenly ten feet tall.

"I was well content having both granddaughter and grandson. But the girl child who went away has come back a man. Is this, then, the kind of magic the white school teaches?" Sparks seemed to flash through the air in the stillness that followed her words.

But the piercing caw of a crow finally shattered the silence, and the girl went in and changed back to Navajo clothes.

The time came around for moving the sheep to new pasture, so early one morning Little Eagle and his mare started off. In bright shirt and levis, he rode without any saddle, with a face so glowing it paled his red head band. Black Star, with her light passenger, stepped in pride and beauty and even Taggo ran ahead like a lively young dog.

"He puts on the show for you," the shepherd told his pony, as he reached up to give her mane a proud caress. It hung now in rippled waves from the sister's braiding. "But you'll see his tail drag long before we've ever reached camp." As he rode, the boy sang the travel song for good luck that he'd learned from his father and grandfather long ago.

They entered a flat world of rock and sage and worked across it, then herded the sheep through the wash to its farther side. They had gone far beyond Grandfather's *chindi* place before crossing. But as he looked back to watch Taggo rounding up the stragglers, Little Eagle's eyes caught a glimpse of the far-off spot. Worse yet, he had seen the side where the hole had been cut—the north side. Toward the north was the way for removing the dead—the way of evil.

Hurriedly the boy made a chant from the Moving Up Way ceremony—the chant that protects from the evil of ghost sickness.

Then the eerie silence was broken by *Doli* the bluebird. From the rabbit brush came his morning song of the dawn. Now the fear that had struck the boy began to lessen, for the happiness bird surely meant that no harm would come.

Suddenly all the world was dressed in sunrise colors. Around the boy on his mare vast orange rocks rose to the sky. Farther on they turned to a lighter shade of yellow and made a golden roof where they jutted out over the trail. When the trail narrowed, boy and dog worked slowly together to send the sheep through the bright and narrow pass.

At the place of the cairn in the creviced side of the canyon the boy drew rein and slid from the back of his mare. This place was sacred, for here Nayenezgani the hero slew a monster that threatened the Earth People long ago. Little Eagle took from his shirt the prayer feather with turquoise and placed it beside the other gifts in the shrine. Then he prayed to both twins of the Sun and his Turquoise Woman:

> Everywhere I go myself
> May I have luck.
> Everywhere my close relatives go
> May they have luck.

From the height of the rock he leaped with feathered lightness again onto the back of his Black Star. A canyon wren trilled a good-by with his sad, sweet song.

But the boy's song was joyful as he again burst into singing, for it was a day when all of the earth seemed glad. Even Black Star stepped as though keeping time to his music, and the tumbleweeds danced as they rolled to the base of the cliffs. Then the mare began running races with the cloud shadows. A jack rabbit watched from the gray-green chamise as they flew. "Ya-ta-yei!" Little Eagle called out to the bright-eyed creature.

At the top of the long high plateau he halted his pony and got down and looked far off where the land met the sky. Below him wide spaces filled up with blue between mesas, and round domes, like brown ant hills, lay scattered widely apart. These domes were the roofs of hogans, the homes of his tribesmen. From them coils of smoke curled out and up toward the sky. It seemed that everything good of the earth reached upward. Even coyote's nose, when he sang, lifted to the sky. Then a buzzard came near. But he was floating downward, for this feaster on death had his eyes fastened low to the ground.

Little Eagle was walking now, leading his pony, and

thinking about those things of the earth and sky. Why was it, he wondered, that some creatures walked and stumbled, while others soared over the world and knew how to fly? And still others swam, some crawled? It was a great mystery. He was pondering it still when he came to the valley below. It was then he was startled by Black Star's neigh from behind him.

From a jut in the lowland there came an answering neigh, then a well-known voice called out a "Ya-ta-yei!" It was Johnny-Runs-Backwards who came riding hard on his pinto. Like a flash Little Eagle was back on his own Black Star. With a whoop and a yell the sheep-herders raced toward each other. And their ponies behaved as though they, too, were old friends.

"Well now," said Little Eagle, "one would think they were of the same clan."

"Or sweetie-sweeties," said Johnny-Runs-Backwards with a wide grin. The baseball cap Johnny wore on his head looked too little, but the smile on his face covered all of Navajoland.

"Ei-yie, but you surely have there a handsome pony," Johnny said with real joy that his friend finally had a horse.

Little Eagle swelled up till he felt big as three Uncle Montys. His head seemed to be floating with the clouds in the sky. "She is Black Star. See here, where she wears the treasured marking." And he pointed out to his friend the four-pointed star.

Young Johnny, quite speechless, beheld the star and marveled. "Not till now," he said, "have I seen this kind with a spot. And to have this marking, indeed it is a wonder!"

They both decided the mare had been sent by the gods.

The two young friends quite forgot that the day was passing in the pleasure of having each other's company. First they ran foot races, then tried to race their ponies. But this they finally gave up in laughing despair. Black Star and the pinto were much too charmed with each other to do anything but run along side by side. So the boys gave in to the whims of their lovesick ponies and decided instead on a game of chicken pull.

They buried the red baseball cap of Johnny-Runs-Backwards, all but its bill. This would serve as the chicken they lacked. Then with whoops and yells they rode wildly toward each other, swooping low to try to grab the cap as they passed. When Johnny fell head-first, both rolled on the ground with laughter. Then suddenly they realized the sun had left them behind.

Little Eagle sat up in dismay. Ahead lay the bad-lands. But now he couldn't thread through them before darkness fell. Navajos almost never went about alone after nightfall, and those shadowed arroyos were not even pleasant by day. Ghosts and witches dwelt in their deep and hidden places.

"Stay with me tonight," said his friend. "Let us make camp together. I know of a place. It isn't much farther on."

So they rode ahead and in no time at all they found it—a hollowed out spot among rocks where a juniper grew. The lone tree's gray roots came out of the ground all twisted, but its limbs served well for hanging their bridles and bows. In a crevice of rock a trickle of water bubbled, so they followed its source and came to a tiny spring. Together the boys made camp and unloaded their ponies, then led them to water and gathered brush for their fire.

"Hot coffee will taste good," Little Eagle said, "and it will warm us, for already the heat of the sun begins to fade."

He had started to hobble Black Star, but Johnny told him there wasn't the need. "She is sure to stay by my pinto, who comes when I whistle." So their mounts were left free to nibble and wander about.

The meal turned out to be quite a feast of corn bread and mutton ribs, which were already cooked but cold. So they put them on sticks and heated them over the campfire. They also had canned peaches that Johnny had brought.

"I borrowed them from my mother's supply in her store-box," he said as he took the can from his saddle bag.

"How glad I am that she let you have these peaches," Little Eagle said, dipping into the can for more.

"It wasn't exactly as though she told me to take them. She just happened to look off the other way when I did." Johnny's round, fat face wore a grin like a he-wolf devil. They laughed and took turns drinking off the juice in the can.

Little Eagle gathered up the bones and scraps for old Taggo. But he found the dog doing quite well enough for himself. That one who would never harm sheep even though he were starving was having a feast on a meal of prairie dog. "You may not be so lucky again to-morrow, so I'll save these scraps for you," he told his dog.

Young Johnny had spread their blankets and sheep-skins by the campfire so the two stretched out and lay looking up at the sky. "Once more Sun Bearer is back with his Turquoise Woman and has hung his sun on a peg in her turquoise house," said Johnny, and both watched as Sky Father slowly pulled twilight's curtains. Then they turned to wrestle and joke and talk till dark.

When stars popped out, one by one, the herders grew quiet. "I wonder what makes them sparkle and shine so bright," said Little Eagle.

"It's because they are made of mica," answered Johnny-Runs-Backwards. "It's the mica that makes stars shine and give off the light."

"First Man put them there," Little Eagle mused. "Coyote helped him. Stars were needed because the moon does not shine every night. First man drew a plan in the sand. For stars he used mica. Then he and Coyote tossed the big pieces up in the sky."

"It's lucky they stuck in the places where they were intended." Johnny's voice sounded drowsy, as though he was far away.

"Only big pieces did," said still wide-awake Little Eagle. "After that, Coyote grew lazy and blew on the rest. They stuck in the sky all right, but not with a pattern. That's why there are so many stars that have no name."

But now from the other sheepskin came only silence.

"*Ahalani*," Little Eagle said to his sleeping friend.

But it was no use. Young Johnny had quit for the night.

"They never did have a name," Little Eagle murmured. And then the stars were no puzzle to him any more. He was back home again with his mother and father and sisters, and all stood around by the side where the squash vines spread. He was helping his mother pick turquoise out of the squashes. And Little Echo, the baby, was tossing them up in the sky.

Little Eagle awoke at the very first bird sounds of morning. He sat up and rubbed his eyes and looked about. *"Ahalani,"* he said to still sleeping Johnny-Runs-Backwards. He had to say it four times to awaken his friend.

"Well now," said Johnny, raising up on an elbow, bewildered, "have you sat there and talked and talked the whole night through?"

"I guess not, for I dreamed I was picking turquoise squashes, and I've never seen any of such a color, have you?"

They laughed and arose, but gathered their bedding slowly—saddened now that time had come for them to part. After packing and drinking the rest of last night's coffee, they mounted their ponies and went their separate ways.

"Go in beauty," Little Eagle called out to Johnny-Runs-Backwards.

"Go in beauty," returned his bright-shirted, red-capped friend.

Little Eagle now herded his sheep in open plains country that showed lava beds where the earth monsters had been slain. The dried lava was their blood, Singing Willow once told him. They were slain by the sons of the Sun and his Turquoise wife. These twins always had been friends to the Navajo people.

The boy said a good luck prayer as they entered the badlands, but once out of that dismal stretch he broke into song. Then he and Taggo began working the higher country, toward the endless stretches of mountains that lay ahead. Good grazing was there, high up in those mountain pastures where aspen and pine and oak and spruce trees grew. Already the tablelands which cut through the valleys were trimmed with the greens of the pinyons and junipers.

Little Eagle was walking now and leading his pony as his eyes searched for plants that his grandmother might need. He gathered and put in his pouch the leaves of the sumac, which the Old One would grind and boil in dyeing her wool. His grandmother knew how to mix the red of the sumac with the gum of the pinyon to get a deep rich black. She had many secrets for making rugs of beauty and never used dyes that were sold at the trading post. The sumac was also used on skins by his father in tanning hides for their bedding needs or for moccasins.

At a patch of juniper scrub he pulled up a root. The lining of juniper roots were used to make red; the berries themselves made dye of a dull blue shade. He hoped he would see some rock lichen for the green. It would make a fine present for Grandmother on his return, for rock lichen wasn't always easy to find. As he walked and searched he chewed on a piece of dried meat.

It wasn't late when Little Eagle reached the sheep camp. A spotted fawn stood munching leaves by the brush corral. It arched its long neck at the sound of Black Star's coming, then bounded away to the shelter of forest trees. In the camp everything was the same as the family had left it. Some hay for his pony still lay in the storage dugout.

But the place seemed so lonely without them—so very silent. Yet he knew that all of the others would soon arrive. First his father would come, bringing with him their needed provisions. Then very shortly, the rest of the family, too, all but the Old One. She would stay to look after the growing things. For this, there must always be one to remain behind.

# CHAPTER VII

# The Blessing Way

IT WAS FIVE DAYS BEFORE GRAY WOLF ARRIVED, AND HE came then only to take Lone Eagle back home. A ceremony was needed after all, and the whole family must be present for Blessing Way. Gray Wolf had brought the lazy Ned-Jo Red-Eye. For three fine sheep Ned-Jo would tend their flock.

There had been no further talk of a Blessing Way when Little Eagle had left to move the sheep. But trouble must have come while he'd been absent. He knew it as they went their homeward way, for Gray Wolf did not talk much as they traveled and wore a face shut off in deep hard thought.

At last the sheepherder, braving his father's silence, said, "Well now, my elder sister, how is she?" He said it as though speaking of the weather.

Gray Wolf, on his black horse, looked off; then said, "I do not know, for seldom does she speak, or sing at all these days. She only dreams. She seems no longer like a Navajo, but wanders in and out or far away."

"My father, is it of the school she dreams?"

"How can I know? I have no way to tell. Sometimes I think perhaps she has a sickness. But then again, she seems to feel quite well."

Yet when they came in sight of home, the family seemed to be at peace and very much the same. Grandmother carded wool over in the coolhouse while Laughing Rainbow sewed out in the sun. Her feet were running races on the pedals of the sewing machine that purred its sewing song. His mother made a dress for Singing Willow of velvet brought back from the trading post. When they had brought Black Star for Little Eagle, they had brought the cloth to make the sister glad. His sister dried her hair now by the grindstone. The baby, Little Echo, chased her lamb.

The corn had grown. The squash vines crept much farther, but there were no blue turquoise on them yet. Little Eagle smiled, remembering his dream. Perhaps to dream of turquoise meant good fortune since The People always wore the stones for luck.

The Blessing Way's first night was mostly singing. It started with the sprinkling of the meal. *Hatali* rubbed a little at the doorway, at its south side, stretching high to reach the top. Then, carrying the basket with the cornmeal, he traveled around the room the way the sun goes and made the gift in silence to the house. From west to north he sprinkled holy cornmeal; and on the floor where timbers joined the ground, with a prayer this time for joy to dwell within. With another prayer he tossed some in the fire, then toward the ceiling, speaking to the Sun:

> Accept this gift, O Bearer of the Day,
> And may it bring delight unto this house.

At last *Hatali* halted at the doorway and sprinkled

white cornmeal out toward the east.

> May this road ever bring light to this hogan
> That peace and harmony may dwell within.

Each day a new sand painting was created to show the stories of the Ancient Ones. The kinsmen of the family also gathered and helped in making paintings with the sand. They made them right out on the hogan's earth floor. Containers made of bark held all the colors, the white and blue and yellow and the black. These colors were made from meal and ground up flowers, and pollen and the powdered minerals too. *Hatali* and his helpers drew the pictures by sprinkling the color with their hands while holding it between their thumbs and fingers.

And on the painting there came Changing Woman, for many of the songs were given by her. At no other time may she ever be shown save on sand paintings made in Blessing Way. Then vividly the other things appeared—the corn and beans and squash and tobacco —for these four plants are sacred to The People. One of the four dry paintings pictured Big Fly and Gila Monster and the Corn Beetle. And one showed stars and mountain animals, and then the bluebird, which means happiness. On each day's painting Rainbow always came around the picture on all sides but east. This was to shield it from the Evil Ones.

Little Eagle knew the Blessing ceremony had been given The People by the Holy Ones. They made man and then taught him skills and rituals for keeping harmony within his life. These legends, songs and prayers told of the creation of earth and sky and sacred

mountains too. And they told of how the moon and stars were placed there, and the way to make the he- and she-rains fall.

The second day was Singing Willow's suds bath of yucca blessed and gathered properly, and the great *Hatali* sprinkled her with pollen and tied a white shell in her gleaming hair. The songs and prayers continued until nighttime, and all night long until the break of day.

Then with the fourth day's close of all the singing and annointing with the pollen and the meal *Hatali* said, "In beauty it is finished." Four times he said, "In beauty it is finished," and the Blessing Way was finally at an end.

Already, on the fires outside the hogan, the kinswomen were roasting mutton ribs. Squash and beans boiled in the big pots all together, and thin corn cakes fried, sizzling in the fat. The delicious smell of desert sage and cooking was almost more than Little Eagle could bear.

But finally all the pots and pans were emptied. And when the fires had died down to a glow, and all the jokes and gossiping and feasting were finished and the kinsmen going home—the sheepherder, asleep up against the hogan, still held a mutton rib clutched in his hand.

With peace once more restored to Gray Wolf's household, there came a blessing from the Water Gods. The washtub was placed underneath the smoke hole to catch the rain that fell inside the house. It rained so hard Little Eagle did not start out to join the sheep back at their far-off camp.

For two whole days the summer storm continued, but inside the home was peace and warm content, for Singing Willow now was well and happy. She never spoke again of white men's ways. She even let the baby sip her coffee, and she made a rag and woolen doll for her. For the doll's hair she made braids out of black sheep's wool.

For her brother Singing Willow had a scarf. It was meant for her, she told the family shyly, blushing and giggling behind her hand. Her good friend Jenny's brother gave it to her as a good-by present when she left the school. Then she showed Little Eagle how to tie the blue scarf around his neck just like their uncle did.

Suddenly the boy felt too tall for the hogan. His head would need the smoke hole to get through. Laughing Rainbow said, twinkling, "My son shoots upward like the sapling that outgrows its mother tree."

It was true. At twelve, he now came to her shoulder, and his levis barely reached below his knees.

"He's going to be big like our Uncle Monty," Singing Willow said.

It was then the sheepherder knew. He stretched up taller still and told them proudly, "Yes, I shall be big like Monty Blue Mountain. And so my name shall also be called Blue. From this day on, I am to be Blue Eagle." The family, agreeing, nodded their assent.

Soon a rainbow came, then sunshine, so Blue Eagle, wearing his new scarf, set out again for camp.

In that bright world that always follows rainfall the boy's light heart lent lightness to the mare. This time she proudly wore a burnished saddle—a gift from Uncle, gotten in a trade.

By the wash the peach trees now had little peaches and, already, one or two were turning pink. They made Blue Eagle think of Singing Willow, and he leaned forward and said in Black Star's ear, "You weren't so maiden shy with Johnny's pinto."

Then he laughed and burst into his travel song and rode with joy, his elbows flapping winglike, the way that Indians always seem to ride.

As Black Star climbed the last rocks toward the camp-site, Blue Eagle saw there had been an accident. A baby lamb had fallen from a ledge.

Yet, up at camp he found far worse disaster: Dead sheep, their bodies lying everywhere. Ned-Joe, that idle, shiftless, ill-begotten, had let them stray where deadly milkweed grew—had let them graze the far plain with its milkweed that is so green and poisonous to sheep. They should have been sent flying from that pasture so fast they had no time to stop and eat. There must be at least fifty dead—all scattered.

He turned away. He could not bear to see. Taggo, the old but faithful, went off limping as though he felt himself to be at fault. But the boy had seen the tear along his shoulder from a battle with the spotted mountain cat.

Blinded by sudden tears of rage and anguish, Blue Eagle raced up to the brush corral. The sight of Ned-Joe leaning on the log pile and chewing on a straw between his teeth made Blue Eagle's hate almost shut off his breathing. His words shot out between great choking gasps. "You'll get no sheep from us, you Child of Hunger! Be gone from here and take your evil too!"

Ned-Joe's hands changed to fists as he came forward. He stood two heads above the sheepherder. But he paused before the other's towering fury, then turned and slinking, snickering, went away.

In despair, Blue Eagle leaned against the log pile. How would he tell the family of this loss? Without those sheep how could they live through winter? What would they eat? And now what should he do? But Taggo had been hurt. He must go find him.

When he'd finally found the injured dog he said, "It's not your fault, my Taggo, have no sorrow." And he stooped to look more closely at the wound.

With herb leaves from the buckskin bag he carried, he made a poultice for the ugly tear. Then speaking soothingly and very gently, he drew the flesh together with his hands. From around his neck he took the scarf he treasured to wrap and hold the healing leaves in place.

"You would have been much wiser not to tangle with the one who walks so softly for his meal. The dead and dying did not need defending. But do not fret. I think the wound will heal. But you must lie here quiet and not move it," he told the dog, who seemed to understand.

Then Blue Eagle made a curing prayer for Taggo and all night long stayed by the sheep dog's side. Four times through that long night he changed the poultice, and waited for the coming of the day.

# CHAPTER VIII

# At the Sweathouse

ON THE RETURN, BOTH BOY AND DOG RODE THE PONY, Taggo bound by a blanket to a strip of wood much like a baby on a cradle board, with the lead sheep on a rope coming behind.

When halfway home, Blue Eagle met his father. Gray Wolf had not come with them earlier, for he'd been busy working on a bridle, a silver order for the trading post. Now he went toward camp to bring back sheep for payment to the medicine man who made the Blessing Way. Gray Wolf had paid *Hatali* thirty dollars but had promised him the thirty sheep as well.

Silently he heard Blue Eagle's tale of sorrow, then turned his horse about to go back home. He had planned to bring the sheep back for *Hatali*, then take all of the family to the camp. But there was no longer need for camp this summer; the sheep that now remained were far too few. Black Star had cost them many, then the poison, and now the medicine man must have his pay.

Even had *Hatali* been the patient's kinsman, a payment for the rite must still be made, else the cure might turn out not to be effective. With heavy hearts the man and boy returned.

But summer traveled on with rains, then blue skies. The pumpkins, like great orbs of orange sun, lay on their vines by blue and yellow corn. And peach trees under cliffs of red and copper grew heavy with their golden rosy fruit.

Laughing Rainbow and the Old One pitted peaches and dried them on some rocks out in the sun. Singing Willow helped to store away the peaches in all the pots and jars she could find.

Blue Eagle and his sheep dog, who was well now, were out again in pasture near the home, for the rains had brought new greenness for the grazing; at least enough to feed so small a flock. As the boy followed the sheep over the mesa a trouble often clouded his young brow. All the family was worried over Elder Sister, who paled and seemed to slowly waste away. In spirit she was once again *hozoni*—at least, content again with Navajo ways—but in her great dark eyes there was a longing that seemed to draw away her very life. Blue Eagle's throat hurt, thinking of her sadness. It was as if she had an ache inside, but she had grown so gentle and so helpful, as though she was trying to hide it from their eyes. What could it be that Elder Sister wanted? It wasn't to be back at school again. Once he had overheard his mother ask her. They were talking when they thought he was asleep.

"My daughter, are you ill?" said Laughing Rainbow.

"No, my mother, I am well," his sister said.

"Then do you wish to be back with the white ones?"

"Nor do I have such sickness in my head. Your words are strange. Am I not of The People? I could never wish to live another way."

So sadness came to live inside the hogan, for no one seemed to know where healing lay.

Blue Eagle leaned against a juniper and whittled on a prayer stick in his hand. Beside him lay four turkey feathers, waiting to adorn the stick cut from a cottonwood.

Suddenly he thought of something. He remembered! Quickly he placed two fingers for the whistle, then grinned with pride to see Black Star respond.

"On the first one that time. You learn fast," he told her, as the frisky mare came romping to his side. "Watch the flock," he called to Taggo, then with one leap he was on Black Star's back and flying home.

But his father wasn't there, he was with Uncle. They were at the sweathouse, Laughing Rainbow said. The hidden sweathouse down below the hogan was the place for cleansing, but sometimes the men just went there to be rid of interference from womenfolks and talk among themselves, and to have their jokes and solve the family problems.

Like the wind Blue Eagle raced down to the hollow to the sweathouse. It was only a little hut, low and wattled, like a hogan only smaller and with no hole at top or any place but the opening that one entered and came out by. The men were coming out now, dripping wet. Dirt and sweat on them were mixing all together as they talked and rubbed themselves with desert sand.

They didn't even see panting Blue Eagle, for they were breathing quite as hard as he, and their eyes were almost shut from all the sweat that ran in little rivers from their heads. They kept on talking while they rubbed the sand on. Talk, talk! Sometimes both men

talking at once. And even when they finally saw Blue Eagle, who was just about to burst with news to tell, they looked right through him. Uncle Monty said, "It is too long a time to wait till first frost to hold either Yeibichai or Mountain Chant."

"My uncle—"

"Night Way and Mountain Top Way both cost money —or sheep—and neither can I spare. I'm puzzled now how we will eat all winter," Gray Wolf replied.

"My father—"

"I think a squaw dance might be just the answer," the big man said.

"My uncle—"

"Neither summer chants nor winter chants are free."

Blue Eagle waved his arms to make them see him, but he might as well have been a rock or tree, for again the men were speaking both together. He had never heard his uncle talk so much.

He wished they had on shirts or at least something that he could yank and make them stop and hear of this thing that would cure Singing Willow's sickness and bring *hozoni* in their home again. But both wore less than jay birds when they hatch.

Then the men ducked back again into the sweathouse for the second steaming that would end the bath. Blue Eagle kicked the sweathouse in frustration. If he'd had an axe he would have chopped it down. Then he tore his clothes off, ripping all the buttons, and like an angry hornet, dashed inside.

The men had finished with the sacred songs which must always be sung when one takes a sweatbath. But it's hard to sing, it's even hard to breathe, in that steam made from wet grass and weeds on hot stones. Still Blue Eagle tried his best to make them hear.

"My father—and my uncle—" he began. But it was no use. Each time his mouth came open, the steam flew in and made him cough and gasp.

When he turned green and almost fell unconscious, his uncle finally pulled him back outside. Gray Wolf came shortly after. He was gleaming, and so was Uncle, for they now were clean. Their bodies shone and glistened like new copper.

"What were you yelling about in all that steam?"

"I'm trying hard to tell, but you won't hear me."

"What you got to say?" his uncle said. He said it in the English. Sometimes he would forget and speak that way.

Blue Eagle told them quickly. He wasn't taking any chances now. "I think I know what would make Sister happy. I think she has a longing for a door."

They looked at him as though he'd lost his senses.

"What would she do with it?" his father said.

"She'd put it where the blanket now is hanging. She wishes for a door like Jenny Chee's."

His father almost laughed. Monty Blue Mountain looked toward a tree and slowly scratched his head. Then both men turned away and started dressing, and he knew they thought he didn't make much sense.

"You may be right," Gray Wolf told Uncle Monty. "A woman needs a man and little ones."

"Yes, a man and children keep a woman happy," Uncle Monty said. They finally had agreed.

72

Blue Eagle felt as useless as a cornstalk that has grown tall but not produced the grain. They'd dusted off his plan for helping Sister as though his words had been "it's going to rain."

Three days passed by before Monty Blue Mountain came back again. He'd been scouting over trails and roads and highways to find a fitting present for his niece. And he had finally found the thing he wanted. Blue Eagle's words were valued after all, for his uncle brought a door for Singing Willow—a door that was of wood like Jenny Chee's.

Already he had shaped the wood and cut it to fit the hogan's doorway—almost fit. It was still a bit too big, so Uncle Monty just propped it up against the doorway's sides. It didn't close and open like that Jenny's— one had to move it to go in and out—but it stood there like the entrance to a fortress, and it bore designs which Uncle said were words. Uncle Monty couldn't make out all the reading, but he knew the last word, which he said was "home."

"H-O-M-E spells home and that means hogan," he told the family gathered round about. Laughing Rainbow nodded, for the word seemed fitting. Many Rivers looked to be somewhat in doubt. Gray Wolf was not around, nor Singing Willow. The girl had gone out for a walk again. By the time she returned, the door had been forgotten, for the others were talking of something else by then.

When she saw the big thing and its lettering, she seemed astonished. "HEAVENLY REST FUNERAL HOME," she read. Blue Eagle beamed. His sister could say all the reading. There was no end of knowledge in her head. Then she turned toward Uncle, looking rather puzzled. "A sign like that was on the road to Gallup. I saw it when our school went in the bus."

But Uncle Monty didn't even hear her, for he was telling of the news he'd learned. This very night a squaw dance ceremony was beginning on a mesa far away. The second night the rite would be much closer, since all the men rode on this way each day. The third and final night they would be dancing at Five Bent Pinyons, just two mesas off. On horseback it would be one half day's journey; in Uncle's truck it would be even less. Uncle thought now was the time for Elder Sister to go and learn to do the Indian dance.

"Already I know how to do the squaw dance," she told him, "for I learned it as a child. I played it like a game with my girl cousins."

"Good, good," said Monty Blue Mountain in English. Since he often mixed his talk with this and that, the family also had picked up some English, which the Old One didn't like to hear. She frowned. Still Uncle Monty kept on with his talking, and soon his plan had Grandmother's consent.

But Laughing Rainbow wasn't in agreement. "My girl is still too young," she said softly. "She is now only in her sixteenth summer."

Blue Eagle thought his mother sounded sad. Then suddenly he understood the reason. To get his sister married was the plan, for he well remembered all that sweathouse talking about how much a woman needs a man.

But now that Singing Willow had her fine door she didn't need to have a husband, too. Both door and husband! Uncle must be loco. What need was there for any husband plan?

# CHAPTER IX

# The Matchmaking

WHEN PARENTS TAKE A YOUNG GIRL TO A SQUAW DANCE, it means the girl is now of marriage age. To attract a man the family thinks is worthy it helps to make a showing of one's wealth. So once again they pulled down all the hard goods from the eaves along the hogan's cribwork roof, and the family dressed up in their finest clothing, not just their own but borrowed finery too. Both Uncle Monty's wives had loaned their jewelry—bracelets, beads and rings, and one fine silver belt.

Singing Willow was so laden with the turquoise, copper, silver, coral, jet beads and white shell that Blue Eagle thought she'd have no strength for dancing. The jewelry covered almost all her dress. It was the velvet blue one that her mother had made for her with such fine skill and care.

Blue Eagle wore a pair of brand new levis. By now he had outgrown the buckskin pants, but the handsome overblouse that Many Rivers had woven long ago and made too big fit him with perfection. How he preened and strutted! Excitement and the fun of preparation had made him lose his dislike of the plan.

When everyone was finally dressed and ready, Many Rivers made a final check to see that each had on his person the protection that must be worn in large gatherings. The little sack of gall The People carry, or wear, is medicine to keep them safe from "corpse poison" when they go where there are strangers. To be sure, four times she made them look and see. Each time all had their witches' remedy.

As the family traveled toward the ceremony, Blue Eagle felt his head would touch the sky if he hadn't been inside the truck with Uncle—he and Father. All the women rode in back. But in the cab he still could hear their voices—Laughing Rainbow's, Many Rivers', Uncle's wives'. Even Singing Willow now joined in their laughter. Little Echo simply squealed out her delight.

"My father, why do people call it squaw dance? Grandmother says it is the Enemy Way."

"The squaw dance is the name the white men gave it."

"But don't The People say 'the squaw dance' too?"

"Yes, now most everybody calls it squaw dance, but in the old days it was Enemy Way. They made the ceremony for the warriors when they returned from fighting and the raids. It kept the braves from getting the ghost sickness from ghosts of enemies that had been slain. But now, since Navajos do no more fighting with Mexicans or other warring tribes, The People sing it to prevent diseases. The alien sickness is the enemy."

"Grandmother says a witch may cause an illness."

"Sometimes an evil witch lies at the cause. But mostly trouble comes in from the outside, like when a Navajo will wed another who is not also of The People's tribe.

The patient of this three-night ceremony is a worker in an Indian agency, in the laundry where he handles white men's clothing and that of sick. He needs to have the Sing for protection from the evils he encounters."

"Will they sing for him tonight?"

"They have already. The first night starts off with the singing chant in a hogan made just for the ceremony."

Blue Eagle had been taken to the dancing before, when he was much too young to care. Like the small one, who would very soon be sleeping, he had also slept through all the revelry and had never given thought to its real meaning, for he had been too young to understand. But now that he'd grown older and much wiser, his questions bubbled like a mountain spring.

"Is this the night that they will have the battle?"

"No, that was last night."

"Father, what's it like?"

"Well, a group of Navajos ride off together to another hogan several miles away. The one whose horse is fastest takes the parcel. Most often it is tied on to a pole. If they think a witch is the reason for the trouble, then the parcel holds something the witch would wear, like a piece of hat, the part that holds his sweating. It must be little, sometimes just a hair. As the riders get near to the second hogan, another group, and these on horseback too, meets up with them. The two groups have a battle, not real of course. It's only just pretend, but it makes the trouble turn then from the patient and go back to the evil witch again."

Uncle Monty, through this talk, drove on in silence. He never did have very much to say. And now Blue Eagle also rode in silence, for he was thinking of the

Enemy Way of the old days when the warriors went to battle.

Then, quietly, Monty Blue Mountain said, "They made the Sing when I went off to army."

"I well remember it," Gray Wolf replied. "I was too young to go and most unhappy, for I was not much older than my son. The Sing was made for some one hundred fifty. They put the photographs all in a pile before the medicine man, a famous singer. He sang the ancient war songs for the men. Some of the men had gone to join the army, and some worked here at home in airplane plants. Even Navajos who followed white men's Jesus were asked to add their prayers to our tribal chants."

Uncle Monty made no answer, but his silence seemed to say his thoughts had now gone far away, back again into that time he joined the army and went to fight the nation's enemy. For a moment the boy knew the tribal longing of his male ancestors for war and show of might. It had been a long time since he'd even wrestled —not since he camped out with Johnny that night.

Then he got lost in the beauty of the country, for Sky goddess was now busy at her loom. She was spinning sunset fire on sky and mountains. It made white clouds look like pink and fleecy lambs.

But the sun passed on and into early twilight. Yet so quickly does the half-light come and go that already darkness crept around the edges of earth and sky to blacken out the show. One small bit of pink still lingered and then faded, paling slowly in the evening afterglow. It's trying hard to stay and see the dancing, Blue Eagle thought.

In back the talk was stilled for that moment when the night and day change places. Then the truck climbed up and rolled down from a hill where they saw the fire-glow on a far-off mesa, long before their ears could hear the pulsing chant.

From all directions now came many wagons and cars and trucks, like slowly moving ants. Lights of *chidis* threw their beams across the desert, making horses snort and break into a prance as The People came on by the many hundreds for the third-night ceremony of the dance.

They bedded Little Echo on the truck floor, using blankets for her covering and bed. Then Blue Eagle hurried off, for he had spotted a familiar baseball cap of flaming red.

"Well, now," said his friend Johnny, grinning widely, "so you have come to see me do the dance."

Blue Eagle laughed. "I don't think you'll be dancing."

"I will if someone gives me half a chance."

At squaw dances the women do the asking, though they don't ask men by saying it with words. A woman comes up to a man who's standing apart, among a group of other men. She links her right arm with his right arm. This causes them to face in opposite ways. With determination, she then pulls her partner into the circle where the dancing is. She leads the dance, relentlessly and firmly. He has to go wherever she may wish, backwards or forwards, and since they aren't facing, the dancing pair seem most impersonal.

The man should pretend he doesn't like the dancing, but before the woman lets him stop he must pay. In the old days he would sometimes give the woman a white child he had brought back from the raids. Or perhaps a skin or horse or maybe jewelry. But nowadays he almost always pays with some money, and she won't take just a little. If it's not enough she goes on with their dance.

Through the throngs of people milling in the open the boys pressed over to the center space where men stood inside a circle marked with saddles thrown on the ground to make the dancing place.

Girls and women glittered in their splendid jewelry and gaily colored skirts with velvet tops. Most men had short haircuts but still wore headbands and their finest shirts of yellow, blue, or red—even purple. There was almost every kind. Blue Eagle saw just one shirt without color, but that white shirt glistened as if made of silk.

People thronged upon the clearing by the pinyons—mothers, daughters, cousins, clansmen friends, and aunts. Many million acres cover all the country that makes up Indian reservation land, so sometimes an interval of many seasons will pass before two friends meet up again. A squaw dance brings the chance for jokes and laughter or for gossiping and making gifts and trades.

Crowds had gathered round the circle left for dancing, and mothers urged their daughters to go and dance. Some even helped their daughters pick a partner; then the girls would go and link arms with a man. Most didn't seem to need a second urging. Some giggled or made silly moans and sighs, but all finally did go out to join the dancing. All but Singing Willow. She refused to dance. There she sat, her head down like a Child of

Hunger—acting simple, making rabbits with her hands.

But Blue Eagle saw something. He smiled at Sister— that white shirt. Singing Willow saw it too, for she turned pink and got busier than ever with her finger game. Who could that white shirt be?

Both the aunts and his grandmother looked unhappy at having Singing Willow act this way. When Blue Eagle saw his father motion to him, he gladly left the women for the men.

As he went, he noticed out among the dancers one head that bobbed along above them all. Blue Eagle grinned. It was none other than Red-Bottle-Stand-Tall, who liked hospitals.

# CHAPTER X

# A Squaw-Dancing Johnny

BLUE EAGLE WENT TO CHECK ON LITTLE ECHO. HIS FATHER wanted him to go and see if the Little One still slept and was well covered. It would be a wonder if she was asleep, for the din of the "sway-singers" had grown greater, and the joking and loud laughter had increased. But he did find Little Echo sleeping soundly beside her doll. They lay there cheek to cheek.

So he hurried back to stand near to the Singer where he could see close up that "groaning stick" made of wood cut from a tree once struck by lightning. The Lightning People gave to Navajos this "bullroarer" that makes the thunder sound when a Singer twirls it by its thong of buckskin. Turquoise and abalone make its face. With his other hand the Singer shook a rattle. Blue Eagle stood now in an excellent place.

He saw White Shirt "sway-singing" with the others. Not once had White Shirt gone to join the dance. When a girl came up he always paid her right off. He must have lots of money in his pants. Well, if he was waiting for Elder Sister to ask him, he would likely wait all night.

Blue Eagle looked around for Johnny-Runs-Back-wards, but his friend wasn't anywhere in sight. Then the singers stopped to have a little rest, and a white man took this chance to make a speech. He urged The People to support reduction, which was the only way to help the land. Fewer sheep gave thicker wool and grew much fatter, because a small number had more to eat. The ranges had grown poor from much erosion—too many horses, cattle, goats and sheep. When the rains came there was no growth left to hold it. So the water washed away the fertile sand. They must raise only livestock which was useful, and needed, if they wished to help the plan which the government had made for conservation.

"Too many sheep has never been my problem," somebody said. Blue Eagle looked around. "To keep the livestock which I am permitted is harder than to keep my number down."

It was his father, Gray Wolf, who had spoken. His words brought laughter from the group of men. But the man from government went right on talking.

Then someone kicked Blue Eagle on the shin. He spun around all ready to give battle and bumped straight into Johnny's he-wolf grin.

"Come see what I have found," said Johnny, slyly. Blue Eagle gladly followed his young friend, for by now he had grown weary of the talking and wished the singing would start up again.

In a little hollow just below the clearing Johnny led Blue Eagle to a sandy mound where he showed him something big and green and shiny.

Blue Eagle let out with a whistle sound. "Ei-yie, a watermelon and a fat one! It's big enough to feed as much as ten! Where did you find it?"

"It found me," said Johnny. "It lay there in some water in a tub, begging me to save it from a death of drowning. And so I did. Well, come on, let's begin." Johnny stooped and cut the melon with a sharp rock while Blue Eagle's eyes went searching all around.

"How did you get it here? It must be heavy."

"It is, but hunger gave me lots of power. I partly rolled it over from that wagon, the one with red wheels on the higher ground."

"Maybe they were saving it for later feasting," Blue Eagle said. His words were whispered now.

"Why feast so late? It is quite ripe and ready and so is my great big fat appetite." And down went Johnny's head into the melon, a piece so big it reached from ear to ear.

Blue Eagle watched. His mouth filled up with water. He longed so much to have a juicy bite, but still he hesitated.

"Ei-yie," said Johnny, "this is the best one I have had in years." The good pink juice ran down like little rivers from Johnny's double chin and from his ears. Then suddenly he stopped. "Why aren't you eating? Now, Cousin, would you help them make a sin?"

"Who?"

"I don't know, but selfishness is sinning—according to the white man's Jesus Way."

"But we're not white."

"It comes in other colors. A stingy man is not a worthy friend."

"Are these your friends?"

"They're my friends now."

"Well, then, in that case it is quite all right."

They gorged themselves up to the point of bursting, then Blue Eagle struggled to his feet again. "I've had enough. I'm going to watch the dancing. Are you coming?"

"Not until I reach the end."

"Well, I hope you're built for holding all that water. I hear it splashing around on my inside."

He found his family women with long faces. From their looks one didn't have to ask to know that his sister hadn't yet joined in the dancing. He yawned. It must be almost time to go.

The "groaning stick" and singing had increased with a power that seemed to bounce against the sky roof. But the dancers kept on dancing solemnly. The ones who watched seemed to have greater pleasure. Giggles, chuckles, chortles ran around the crowd from everyone except his family of women.

Even White Shirt now had finally joined the dancing. He was quite busy hopping up and down, making dust fly as his partner's skirts flew outwards. Those flying bright skirts made a pretty sight.

"Why don't you go dance with Red-Bottle-Stand-Tall?" Blue Eagle shouted in his sister's ear.

"Bah, that one has no hard goods," said Grandmother, "and fewer sheep if he has flocks at all."

"I wonder," Singing Willow's words came softly as though she didn't mean them to be heard, "if his father knows he came here to this dancing."

But Blue Eagle had caught every single word. "Are you speaking of our friend, Red-Bottle-Stand-Tall?"

Singing Willow gave a start and then replied, "No,

the tall one doesn't even have a father. I speak of one that's son to Mr. Chee."

Suddenly a light flashed on inside Blue Eagle. "Dan Chee, the one that walks the Jesus Way? Is that his son who dances in the white shirt? The same that gave the scarf you gave to me?"

His sister nodded. "Yes, that one is he."

Blue Eagle grinned, full of an inner laughter. Inside his memory pink cheeks and stolen glances, scarf and shyness had added up to solve the mystery.

While the music stopped to give the leading singer time to tell another song and start the beat, Uncle's younger wife now said to Singing Willow, "There was no use in lending you our hard goods. We might as well have worn it on ourselves. And your mother's time and trouble were all wasted in making you those clothes so rich and fine."

Then the sharp, short beat of chanting came again.

Suddenly, with eyes afire and her jewelry gleaming, Singing Willow stood like a princess of the night. Then, without a word, she walked toward the dancing circle, her grace and beauty making the night more bright.

It was just then that Watermelon Johnny stumbled toward the circle. What a sight to see! His stomach stuck out to the point of bursting and his legs were almost buckling at the knees.

Singing Willow, in a flash, latched on to Johnny and dragged him out into the dancing ring. Caught off guard, Johnny-Runs-Backwards seemed bewildered and not aware of what was happening. He stumbled, slid and staggered as she pulled him, then struggled in an effort to get free. But Singing Willow had made her decision and was determined now to join the dance.

Around the crowd of watchers there was laughter at seeing Johnny caught in this trap. But Blue Eagle looked upon the scene with horror. What was his elder sister thinking of? She shouldn't have picked Johnny for a partner. He was too young for her and far too fat.

Johnny's eyes were popping out like two great saucers, for by now he saw that there was no escape and was trying hard to match his partner's dancing. But he couldn't seem to make his legs behave.

There was an even greater roar of laughter as Johnny worked to make his dancing fit with the rhythm. If one gets caught for a partner, it's just as well to make the most of it.

With a misery that was beyond endurance, Blue Eagle looked around to find some help for his sister, who had surely lost her senses. But his women sat in haughty contempt—all but Laughing Rainbow. Though she wasn't smiling, there was a sparkle in his mother's eyes. What was the matter with his family women? He wished he were at home in bed, for he couldn't bear this laughter at his sister as she dragged that red-faced Johnny all around.

But now young Johnny wasn't doing badly. His face had lost some of its fiery heat and his eyes had settled back into their sockets, for his legs had finally found the proper beat. Still, they made an awfully silly looking couple—Singing Willow towering over short, fat Johnny, and Johnny's stomach sticking out ahead.

*90*

"I'm sure he doesn't have a coin to pay her," Blue Eagle thought with panic. From the men came his echo, "Hey there, Johnny, why not pay her? Or don't you even have a copper cent?"

And then, though it was almost past believing, on Johnny's face there came a little smile, for by now he was all finished with the learning and was hopping up and down in excellent style.

He hasn't sense enough to look unhappy. I do believe he quite enjoys himself, thought Blue Eagle.

In the group of men the laughter had grown until it reached a mighty shout. Some were even tossing silver coins and coppers. "Hey, Johnny, here's a dime to help you out."

But wild horses couldn't drag Johnny from dancing now that he had caught on to his partner's swing. His smile had grown into a grin of triumph so wide it seemed to cover the dancing ring. And in his new-found skill he grew much bolder, making fancy hops and kicking extra high.

"You'd better have a care, you stupid rooster, or you're going to strut yourself into a fall!" yelled Blue Eagle.

But his angry words were wasted. Prancing Johnny could not possibly have heard, for the crowd was wild by now. Even the singers were laughing so, they couldn't chant the words, and all the other dancers had stopped to watch this very special sight. For he who had won his name by racing backwards was dancing backwards now in sheer delight.

Not once through all this yelling and commotion did

Singing Willow even slightly smile nor show that she considered it amusing or strange to go squaw dancing with a child. Even when wild Johnny almost kicked her head in, she kept on dancing in the usual style, soberly and solemnly, without confusion.

"I'll never look upon her face again nor call her sister, for that one is shameless and brings disgrace upon the family name," vowed Blue Eagle. Then in misery he looked toward his own women to see if they still managed to survive. He was half prepared to find they had all fainted.

He looked and then stared, stricken with dismay. His mother, aunts, and grandmother were laughing! His sister's shame had proven far too great. They had gone loco! Well, it was better this way, for it spared them from the pain of the disgrace Singing Willow's wantonness had brought upon them. In despair he looked back toward the ring again. They would probably dance on and on forever.

But the strutting rooster now had settled down. More than that. It seemed that Johnny was in trouble, for the red was rising back into his face. And his legs no longer followed Singing Willow's. She almost had to drag him round the place.

The din thinned down, and then became a murmur. What was the matter with the dancing king? people wondered. Johnny seemed to be in anguish. And now his legs refused to do a thing.

All at once his eyes popped out in utter panic. They almost jumped out of his flaming head. With a wild yell he broke loose from Singing Willow and tore off like one fleeing from the dead. Through the night he raced into the darkened desert.

On Blue Eagle's face there came a crafty grin. He knew why Johnny tore off from the dancing. It had been such an excellent watermelon.

# CHAPTER XI

# At the Trading Post

THOUGH THE SQUAW DANCE DIDN'T BRING WHAT THEY expected, for the most part it had been a happy time. It was a night the family would remember, and it hadn't cost them sheep or any cash.

But now their thoughts must turn to matters other than Singing Willow. Summer neared its end and their stock was low. More sheep were badly needed to feed them through the long, bleak winter moons. But if Cold Woman sent the Hunger People, they would meet their suffering with fortitude. And with calmness. The proud nature of The People could face adversity. They would endure.

Soon Gray Wolf left for the far salt deposits along with other clansmen, kin and friends, but the family didn't go on the long journey. It would have meant additional expense.

In his absence Many Rivers' nimble fingers were busy as she sat before her loom. She wove to finish up the rug to trade for the needed sheep to see the family through. Often Singing Willow stood beside the Old One, for her grandmother was teaching her the skill which the Navajos had learned from Spider Woman and Spider Man, who taught them how to weave.

And each day when he came home from the pasture Blue Eagle saw the difference in the rug as it grew in size and softly glowing colors. The Old One's weaving skill was fine and sure. Then came the day when it was finally finished—all but the little place between the threads, just a small slit. This was left to give an outlet for the spirit in the Navajo design.

On the morning that they were to go for trading, Blue Eagle wakened with a prickly skin. Around his head a dragonfly was buzzing. Or was it just a ringing in his ears?

Already Laughing Rainbow had arisen and removed the ashes from the day before and was busy laying juniper and kindling for starting up the early morning fire. But Blue Eagle didn't get up from his sheepskin, for he was thinking of a dream he'd had. During the night he had beheld one now departed. In a dream the spirit of Grandfather came. Prickling skin and ringing ears foretold disaster, but seeing ghosts in dreams was even worse. Maybe this was not a good day for their journey. Still, maybe staying home would not be best. He wished they had the time for divination so he could learn which way the danger lay. Had they done something that angered the Holy People or failed to do some ritual that they should?

He watched his mother move about the hogan and listened closely as she sang the song that was necessary with her daily duty of starting up the early morning fire. He saw her walk with care around the sleepers. To step over someone would bring them ill. No, she hadn't done a thing against the custom. Then gradually

Blue Eagle's fears were stilled as he listened to his mother sing the blessing. Her words fell like soft petals round his ears.

Outside the wooden door he heard *Hostodi,* who made the plaintive sound of whippoorwills. The sweet scent of the juniper rose upward. The day had come.

Singing Willow wasn't going with the family. She offered to remain and watch the flock. Perhaps she thought her brother would forgive her if she stayed at home and let him go instead, for he hadn't yet forgotten how his sister and young Johnny made that awful "turkey-trot."

Uncle came for them and brought his younger wife. But Mother, Grandmother, and Uncle Monty had barely space enough to sit themselves, for Uncle was a man of great proportions, and the back part might have sheep on the return. So Aunt stayed to look after Little Echo, and Blue Eagle rode in the back of the truck alone. Up in front, the lovely rug of Many Rivers lay carefully rolled across the women's laps.

The journey to the trading post seemed endless. By now the land had lost its springtime green and the desert flowers no longer were in blossom. The sun sent down such cruel and angry heat that the back of Uncle's truck could roast a yearling. The very air seemed threatening and still.

But maybe it's because a rain is coming, Blue Eagle thought. He wanted to feel glad like the day that they had traveled to the mission and the rain had come before they reached the school. But that time now seemed as far away as star dust, or the distance from the earth up to the moon. And the wretched heat was making him remember his bad-luck dream. The memory came back strong.

But when they finally reached their destination, the friendly trading post dispelled his gloom. Outside the store some men were playing stick dice. Inside, The People stood around the room or sat on benches; some sat on the floor. Uncle Monty bought four drinks of bottled soda, one for each of them. Its sweet and biting coldness made the boy quickly forget his earlier fears.

The Old One laid her rug upon the counter, then went and sat down on the wooden bench. This was the proper way to do when trading. One shouldn't ever make a deal too soon.

The trader was now busy with a letter that he was writing for one of the men. When he finished, he glanced over at the Old One, then went across the room to see her rug. Blue Eagle knew he saw its fine perfection, but the trader also knew how to pretend, since he was well accustomed to The People and their ways. He laid the rug back down again.

It was going to take a long time for the business, so the young sheepherder looked through all the scarfs stacked in colored piles on top of the candy counter. He found one like the one he'd had before, but for such a little while. It had been ruined when he used it to bind up the sheep dog's wound. Perhaps he might forget about the dancing. Sister hadn't ever been the stingy kind.

A handsome *chidi* stopped outside the store. He never had seen one like this before. How its yellow glistened in the brilliant sunshine! The man who was driving sat in front alone. A woman sat in back. She was white.

"She eats too much," Blue Eagle decided, as he watched the man help her out of the car. Was she crippled? No, she walked like any other. Now both were coming toward the trading post.

Once inside the store the woman stood in wonder, making funny little noises—"ahs" and "ohs." Then she went around looking at everybody as though all were there just for her to see.

The white one's like the *gah*. She won't stay quiet, Blue Eagle thought. And it was very true. The woman hopped about much like a rabbit.

But she stopped in front of the boy's grandmother and stared squarely in the Old One's stolid face, talking all the while in English to the trader or to her driver.

In Navajo the trader said softly, "She thinks the Old One's eyes have become sightless."

A little smile went flitting around the place on the face of everyone but Many Rivers, who didn't even flinch nor turn away. She just looked straight ahead and through the other as though the woman were an empty space.

So the Bouncing One bobbed up to the grocery counter and looked at all the cans and things to eat; next at the harnesses and saddles, then the velvets. She ran her hands through all the leather belts. When her eyes fell on the silver and the copper, the trader laid the trays out on the case.

Well, at last the *gah* is settled, thought Blue Eagle, as the woman fell upon the jewelry things. But now her chattering is like four magpies.

Uncle Monty, who had been outside, returned, for

he always thought this kind of show amusing—and much more fun to watch than stick dice games.

Then the woman, busy talking to the trader, pointed over toward where Laughing Rainbow sat. The trader shook his head at what she asked him. This made her frown. She plainly was not pleased.

"She wants a pair of earrings like your mother's," Uncle Monty told the boy now at his side.

Blue Eagle smiled. She'd never find another like those; they were his mother's special pride.

But the woman kept on talking to the trader, and again he shook his head and told her, "No."

"She wants to buy the earrings from your mother but the trader keeps on telling her 'No dice'," Uncle Monty said, amused. But then he stiffened.

For the overfed one boldly crossed the room and leaned down to look more closely at the earrings. All the laughter fled from Laughing Rainbow's eyes.

Now the woman tried to talk to Laughing Rainbow. Since the trader wouldn't talk for her, she tried. She made signs and gestures, pointing to the earrings, then to herself. "Sell! Sell—to me!" she cried.

When Blue Eagle's mother didn't even answer, it seemed to make the woman angrier still. Her eyes changed and her voice grew even shriller. "Can't these people understand a single word?"

It wasn't what she said but how she said it, and though Blue Eagle couldn't understand, he knew his mother did. She knew some English but never spoke anything but Navajo.

From The People now there came a little shifting,

like a rumble that cannot be heard but felt. The trader came out from behind the counter. Uncle Monty's hand was scratching at his belt.

"She doesn't know my father made those earrings for my mother and her special use alone, with a skill filled full of love when they were courting. He gave them as a payment at the dance on the same night that they both agreed to marry," Blue Eagle said, then saw he was alone, for by now his uncle stood near Laughing Rainbow.

Still the woman went on screeching as before. When she finally stopped for breath, the trader told them, "She offers twenty dollars for the pair." His words in Navajo gave information to all the other watchers in the store. But the mother must have thought the trader meant them for her. She shook her head.

This sign that Laughing Rainbow understood her made the woman more determined now. With finger signals she increased her offer. But Blue Eagle's mother shook her head again. For a while the woman tried hard to be patient, making all her words and gestures loud and slow. But at last she flung her arms upward in anger and turned away, as if she meant to go.

The trader said, "She offers sixty dollars and says she will not pay a penny more."

Blue Eagle wondered at the sudden stillness. Then he saw his mother slowly raise a hand and remove one of her most beloved treasures—then the other one. She didn't show a single sign of sorrow. Just that dull, defeated look clouding her eyes.

He felt as though someone had shot an arrow through

the very place that sent up all his breath. With one flashing bound he stood before his mother and said to her, "This thing you do is wrong!"

Her face was strange. This could not be his mother—not even her voice—the words he heard her say:

"A mother's strength is often like a mountain, but not when her own children are in need. At such times she will trade an honored treasure, or anything to give their hunger ease. Should I wear my earrings while my children suffer, I could never look in their eyes again."

"No, my mother—" he began. But Uncle Monty interrupted. "Go get lost and close your face."

Though the big man's words had been spoken in English, Blue Eagle knew well what his uncle meant, so he shuffled over to the candy counter and pretended interest in the peppermints.

The driver quickly counted out the money for the woman who, the earrings in her hand, now said "thank you" to unseeing Laughing Rainbow, then hurried off to leave the trading post.

It was when she reached the door that Laughing Rainbow also remembered to say "hokkai-shai," but it seemed as though his mother's words of "thank you" were meant to bid her jewels the "beauty way."

When the family finally finished all their business, they climbed into the truck for the return. Again Blue Eagle made the homeward journey riding in the back of Uncle's truck alone, for the trader didn't have the sheep at present. But he would send them on when they came. Many Rivers' trading had been most successful. In exchange for sheep the trader kept her rug.

With Blue Eagle all was once again *hozoni*. His

mother had bought him another scarf, which she paid for with some of her fine new money. And he also had a bag of lollipops. He would share the candy with his little sister after they got home—Singing Willow too.

For a time he stood and held on to the siding of the truck so he could see what lay ahead. It was not so hot as it had been that morning.

"Sun Bearer has already gone to bed, or perhaps he is just resting," said Blue Eagle. "In summer time his working days are long. But I do believe a rain storm may be coming. I can see the rain now way up there ahead." And he laughed because to him it was so funny that every time he journeyed from his home all the rain clouds gathered to give him a wetting. "I guess the rain gods like to play me jokes."

He thought of the new scarf he was wearing, so he laid his sack of candy on the floor, untied the scarf and folded it, then placed it in a corner underneath the sheepskin rug that the women used when riding in the back part. He took one lollipop out of its paper and sat down on the truck's hard wooden floor. As they rode along he ate his stick of candy and listened to the rising of the storm.

# CHAPTER XII

# The Hole in the Wall

IT CAME ON WITH GREAT GUSTS OF WIND THAT WHISTLED and moaned like many people in distress, and it blew the sand about them in such thickness that they couldn't even see the trail ahead. Blue Eagle grabbed the sheepskin for a cover to keep the sand out of his nose and eyes. He stuffed the new scarf down inside his shirt front, along with all the colored lollipops.

A clap of thunder struck against the sky roof with such a noise it must have cracked the sky, for right then the rain began. It came with fierceness, like a mighty army covering the land.

The boy moved back into the farthest corner of the truck and hugged himself up in a ball. But one bright black eye peeped out. The truck was creeping. He wondered that it still could move at all for the Wind and Rain were fighting a great battle. How could Uncle even see the way to drive? If the storm was moving this way from the mesa, maybe Uncle hoped they soon could pass it by.

Blue Eagle's thoughts turned to his elder sister, who was tending sheep for him, out there alone. But maybe she had seen the rain storm coming and had time enough to get the flock back home. Maybe even now the sheep were in their shelter and his sister in the hogan, safe with Aunt.

Then Wind died down. "Rain thinks he's won the battle, so he stops to smoke a pipe and have a rest," the boy thought. "But Rain shouldn't, for the Wind is just pretending. He's only gone to reinforce his flanks."

And in the time that Wind and Rain were resting Blue Eagle saw the country all around. It was filled with water as wide as Sun Bearer crosses to get back home each night to Turquoise Woman, who lives beyond great waters in the west.

They passed a cottonwood that was uprooted and lying on its side, an injured thing. Water dripped like blood beneath its wounded branches which once had sheltered creatures on the wing.

Then Rain returned. Wind, too, came back with fierceness. They might continue on like this all night.

But through the battle Wind and Rain were waging the truck continued splashing on ahead, leaving in its wake great tracks of churning water. Uncle Monty had to turn on all the lights.

Night really came before they reached the hogan—black night—no stars or moon to light the way. Aunt was waiting for them, standing in the doorway. They saw her in the firelight from the room. She was distressed because of Singing Willow, who had gone out long ago and not returned.

"But the sheep are in," Blue Eagle said in wonder. His sister would not walk in dark and rain.

Then his aunt told how the girl had gotten the sheep home and safely penned, then saw that one was gone—one of the lambs. She hadn't missed it sooner because of all the trouble with the storm. Though the aunt had tried to make her wait till later, the girl had dashed right out to find the stray.

"It must have grown afraid of all the thunder," Blue Eagle said. "It hid or ran away." And he filled with pride to know that Singing Willow would venture forth at night in such a storm. This was as it had been before she left them to go and get confused in white men's ways. She was still the one who tended sheep with wisdom and troubled to keep all the flock from harm. How odd that now when Sister was not with them he should feel she had at last come home to stay.

But Laughing Rainbow, who was tired, grew worried. Already she had had a sorry day, and she thought that Singing Willow showed poor judgment. To go out in this storm for just one stray might show her daughter had no lack of courage, but it showed she could use quite a bit more sense.

The grandmother was busy spreading pollen about the place and muttering good luck prayers. But the Old One's years were mounting up in numbers, and she also had had a lengthy day. Soon peaceful sleep had caught her in a slumber that put an end to all her wordless fears.

There was no use in seeking Singing Willow. They didn't even know where to begin. Uncle's truck could not go flying like an airplane. And if it could, they wouldn't see the girl, not even if she stood right there below them. To try to drive would get them stuck in sand if they left the trail.

So Uncle, Aunt, Blue Eagle, and his mother all waited

as they listened for the sound that might tell them Singing Willow was returning. Uncle let the truck lights shine to light her way.

With a start, Blue Eagle wakened out of slumber that had crept upon him stealthily. Uncle, too, lying by the fire, was snoring. Even Aunt seemed to be sleeping peacefully and, of course, the Old One and the baby sister. But Laughing Rainbow still was standing by. All alone his mother waited at the doorway, looking east for signs of light bringing on the day.

Yet the outside world was still wrapped up in blackness. Even Uncle's truck lights now no longer shone. But the rain had stopped. Blue Eagle rose up quickly.

"Do not fear, my mother, I will find my sister, and very soon I'll have her safely home."

"It is dark," his mother said.

"But not for long now. And I feel that she is somewhere very near."

He had told her this because he knew she suffered. But when he was alone upon his mare, then the sheepherder filled with a fearful boding that his sister was no longer anywhere.

"But she must be! Black Star, surely you can find her," he said, and let the pony take the lead, for the night was far too black to try to guide her. He couldn't see his hand before his face.

There was no sound that anything was living, even usual ones from creatures of the night—just the squashing sound of Black Star's steps in soft mud as she went carefully at her own pace.

But it seemed she only took him in wide circles. Still

he couldn't tell. He let her have her way, for he realized now he'd lost the four directions. Mounting fear was making all his senses sway.

He felt an evil coming up behind him—getting ever closer, reaching for his back. Then Black Star gave a snort and shied beneath him as something flitted right across their path.

Wildly, he flung his arms around the pony. The light! Oh, anything to have some light! "Find her, Black Star. You must find Elder Sister. How terrible this night must be for her. Seek out Taggo, your good friend. He's surely with her. If we find him we will find my sister, too."

He didn't know how long, it seemed forever, that he lay there clinging to his pony's neck. He kept his eyes shut tight to keep from seeing all the blackness that was hanging everywhere and tried pretending sleep to hide his terror of the evil that was lurking all about.

He had thought his eyes were closed, but they were open, for he saw his pony's head come into view—very faintly, though, as through great folds of vapor. Then he saw a pale gray dimness in the west. But it must be east. It must be. Dawn was coming!

With joy the boy let go his hold on Black Star and sat up and quickly made his Dawn Boy prayer with a heart that pounded from its heaped up gladness. Warmth and life were racing back into his limbs as gray images came toward him—slowly, slowly—until finally all the desert lay in view, looking dismal, bleak, and beaten from the rain storm. But to the boy it was a splendid sight.

Suddenly Blue Eagle reined his mare up sharply.

Why was the pony taking him this way—toward the *chindi* hogan where Grandfather's ghost was hiding? He signaled for the mare to turn away. "Come now, Black Star, take heed of what you're doing." But Black Star was of a mind to go straight on, and again she started toward the place of evil.

In the black of night they had come far below it and even over on the other side, where they often took the sheep to do their grazing. But now Black Star insisted on her way. She was tossing at the reins and misbehaving and wanting to go on at faster pace. "You are not my horse this morning," said Blue Eagle, and he made the strangely wilful mare obey.

But just as they were turning, the sheepherder pulled rein. "Sho'h, be still!" He had thought he heard something from *that* direction. Yet he wouldn't turn his head to look that way. But again the mare turned around with sudden quickness, and his eyes glimpsed the *chindi* place against his will. He had seen a movement up beside the hogan! By its north side, something black and white and small. Then came again that sound —a quick, high sharpness. It was Taggo, who would seldom bark at all.

Blue Eagle didn't even try to stop her as Black Star went ahead. He was too dazed. And the mare, since she had no more interference, went forward at an easy gait. She seemed to know that any quickening of pace would surely make her master change his mind, for though he sat his mare with eyes wide open, the boy seemed in a dream or kind of spell as the pony carried him toward the *chindi* hogan—closer and ever closer to the place.

Old Taggo, when he saw that they were coming,

nearly tied himself in knots of wagging joy. But why was he not running on to meet them? Blue Eagle wondered. Then the sheepherder saw old Taggo turn and go into the hogan. And he went right through that hole cut in the wall!

On seeing this, Blue Eagle seemed to waken from the strange enchantment that had brought him here to the very brink of unknown, sure destruction. It was also then that Black Star stopped to drink from a muddy water puddle there before them.

The sheepherder was too afraid to move, but his thoughts were in a panic of confusion. What did old Taggo mean? What should he do? His sister wouldn't be inside the hogan. Only witches ever went in such a place.

But while he sat in fear and indecision, there came another sound so pure and sweet that it surely couldn't come from any evil. It was the sound of music, soft but clear.

The boy got down and lay flat on his stomach and slowly—inch by inch—crept toward the place. A few yards from the hogan he stopped. He listened. Now his eyes could see straight through the gaping hole. But all he saw was dirt and dissolution, and the decayed carcass of some animal. Yet, again there came that sound, and it *was* music.

Blue Eagle gave himself no time to think but climbed over and into the *chindi* hogan, for he knew that Singing Willow was within.

She was sitting at one side beneath the rafters. The sleeping lambkin's head was on her knee, but her hands were working with a row of pebbles which she had set out most peculiarly. She didn't even know Blue Eagle watched her until the foolish dog, from sheer delight, began to bark. She looked up then with fright.

But when she saw her brother there above her, she smiled, relieved, and said, "So you have come."

For a moment the sheepherder could not answer. Whatever was his sister thinking of? Here she sat, inside this awful place for shelter! Far better would it be to take a chance with the wind and rain and all the gods of lightning. But by now his earlier fear was almost spent. In its place there rose a feeling of strong outrage. He had gone through *Chindita* last night alone. And now he stood here in this *chindi* hogan! Yet his sister only smiled and said, "You've come."

"Are you not troubled, thinking of our mother, who waits in fear that you have come to harm?" Blue Eagle's face had flushed an angry color.

"I could not come. I found the little lambkin, but I hurt my foot while carrying it home. Since I could not walk, I looked around for shelter, and crawled in here to keep us both from harm."

"In such a place? Where danger is far greater?"

Singing Willow smiled a little as she said, "If the dead were waiting for me with their evil, then my music must have frightened them away."

"But to sing—and to these stones! Our little sister, even she would not behave in such a way."

"My brother, do not think I've lost my senses. I've tried so hard to let this longing go. But it lives in me. I guess it will forever. And it brings something of comfort to pretend." As she spoke his sister's eyes clouded with sadness and shortly they were glistening with tears. Then she said, "Unless I come here for this solace, I think my living days will quickly end."

"You've come before?" Blue Eagle asked in wonder.

The young girl nodded. "Often just to dream. These rocks you see are keys on my piano. My fingers play, the sound is in my head. It's wrong, I know, to hold on to this longing. And yet I wouldn't have it go away. But I often fear I will forget my learning, and so I come to hide myself and play."

"Is this the reason, then, for all your strangeness?" Blue Eagle was amazed.

"It fills my days. But rocks send back no music like the keys of my piano when I play. And sometimes now my head will fail to tell me, and then my fingers lose the beauty way." She sighed and turned away and said with sadness, "If only it were really a piano."

Blue Eagle stood without a word to say.

Then again she turned to him. "But do not tell them. Please promise that you will not let them know. I wouldn't have my mother know my longing—nor the others, since there's nothing they can do."

"I will not tell." Blue Eagle made the promise.

Then he helped his sister through the gaping hole and onto the pony, who had stood there waiting. He handed up the lamb for her to hold. Then he took the reins and led them on and homeward, with the faithful sheep dog trotting at his side. He knew now what was Singing Willow's trouble. Yet he saw no way to bring it to an end.

## CHAPTER XIII

# The Separation

BLUE EAGLE PONDERED ON THIS ALIEN SICKNESS THAT stuck in Singing Willow like a thorn. As he rode about the pasture on his pony, he thought and thought how it might be removed. Yet he knew that even if they were successful in plucking out the thorn, the hole would stay. No, his sister would never be free of longing. It had been that way with him to have his mare.

True, she never went again back to *that* hogan, but now she seldom got up from her bed. Laughing Rainbow's eyes were great with fear and worry, and Gray Wolf almost never spoke at all. He came and went in quietness and sorrow, and his face showed all the dread that gripped his heart, and Blue Eagle knew they were afraid for Sister. Yes, they feared that she might even "go away."

He suffered for his parents and his sister. For he knew so well the anguish each endured. Yet he'd promised not to tell what caused her illness—that piano she had come to love at school. He remembered how it was to have a longing. The longing part was surely bad enough. But to finally find one's treasure—then to lose it . . . Blue Eagle reined his mare at such a thought.

It was the school that did this to his sister—the tearing of her heart between two ways. Now all of her would never be with The People. Yet for her the white man's world would have no place.

He sat a moment, hating all white people. Then a sudden realization made him frown.

It hadn't been the whites that caused his longing. Longings seemed to come in every size and shape and —like Johnny said—in lots of different colors.

He shook his head. A crazy kind of bluebird—this white-man thing his sister longed to have. Still, Navajos used much they learned from white men—like coffee and soda pop and things in cans—even *chidis*.

"When we like a thing, we use it," he told Black Star. And now his face was suddenly alight. "So why should Sister not have her piano if it would bring *hozoni* back again?"

The trouble was, they surely cost much money, and the family didn't have a bit to spare. Laughing Rainbow had even sold her treasured jewels for fear they would all later be in need, and his grandmother had worked her fingers tender to finish up the rug to trade for sheep. But since the flock was small from the disaster, the new ones barely made up for the loss. The flock was also small because they'd traded the finest of their sheep to buy his mare. Yes, the finest of their sheep to buy his mare.

Then Blue Eagle knew he'd found the only answer. By midday he had brought the sheep back home—much too early for the flock to leave the pasture—but his heart had pointed out the way to go, and he knew he must go quickly. Or not ever. So when the sheep were safely in their pen, without a word to any of the family he turned Black Star and rode away again.

Before Gray Wolf had left for the salt deposits he had told the boy that one day very soon he should turn the pony loose to graze in pasture. Maybe his father thought she needed rest, for Black Star wasn't underfed or poorly. Of late she'd even seemed a bit more wide. But the boy was grateful now for Gray Wolf's counsel. It spared him from the need to tell a lie. If the women noticed that the mare was missing, they would only think he'd done what Father said.

At a later time, of course, he'd have to tell. But by then it wouldn't matter to the family, for if his mission turned out as he planned, then *hozoni* would come back into the hogan with the joy that lived in Sister's eyes again.

Night was barely creeping in around the edges when Monty Blue Mountain and the boy returned. Uncle Monty, coming back from Fort Defiance, had passed the trading post and seen Blue Eagle there all alone. The boy had finished with the thing he'd come for. He had even watched them lead away his mare. Then he stood quite lost and emptied of all feeling. When Uncle had called he didn't even hear.

Going home, Monty Blue Mountain had insisted on knowing why he was so far from home. So the boy had had to tell about his sister. He might as well—they'd soon know anyway. But he didn't tell about the *chindi* hogan. That part he skipped for Singing Willow's sake.

"—and I brought the mare to trade for a piano," he said at last.

Uncle made a long *whoosh* sound like wind in a tunnel. After that the big man drove without a word. He hadn't even said the boy showed wisdom. Yet he didn't say he'd done a foolish thing. But by then it didn't matter to Blue Eagle, for the singing that had lived in him had died.

Aunt was waiting when they pulled up to the hogan. Uncle Monty didn't even go inside. He and Aunt continued on. So the sheepherder went in alone and very soon to bed. Laughing Rainbow had his beans and cornbread waiting, but for once Blue Eagle had no appetite.

In the early morning, just as day was coming, he arose and let the sheep out of the pen. Old Taggo ran ahead to tend his charges, and Blue Eagle followed slowly.

The first ray of sunlight on the mountains made him feel an actual shaft of stabbing pain, like an arrow point had used him for a target.

The day moved on and on, endlessly.

When it was only halfway through its journey, the boy and sheep dog turned the flock about. Blue Eagle had no heart this day for herding, and his legs seemed strangely tired and all worn out. "I guess they're just not used to so much walking," he said out loud. "Black Star, you've made me soft." He had spoken just as though the mare were with him.

Then he stopped to rest upon a jagged rock. He sat so quietly that Gila Monster crawled up and sunned himself right by his side, and the sun was going down behind the mountain before the boy had hardly moved at all.

Twice old Taggo came, wagging, to tell his master it was past time to turn the sheep around. So at last the boy stood up and gave the signal. "Okay, go start old Cross-Eye with his bell." But when he rose the dog had bounded forward and was already at the lead sheep's heels. Blue Eagle smiled wanly. That was a smart one. Lots of zip and sizzle in old Taggo yet.

He spat. Then saw that a cloud of dust was rising in the distance. It was headed toward his home. Perhaps Grandmother's sheep were now arriving. If he hurried he could help them to unload. But such a lot of dust for just one *chidi*?

Then Blue Eagle saw that there were several more. Maybe it was Father and the kin and clansmen who had journeyed for the salt arriving home. It *was* Gray Wolf! He rode with Uncle Monty in Uncle's truck. Red-Bottle-Stand-Tall too. And behind them came the others, all returning.

Blue Eagle's heart picked up its beat again. It had been a long time since he'd seen his father. He tried to drive the sheep at a faster pace, for the caravan already was arriving. Then Singing Willow came to lend a hand after she had greeted Gray Wolf and the others. She took the flock so he could run ahead.

All the women were outside to meet the travelers. Behind his uncle's truck were parked four others and a trailer. In the last one sat the trader, who now got out and came to greet the boy.

In the trailer of his truck was something covered, Could he have brought the piano so soon? Behind the boxlike thing stuck out the head of—it was—*it was his mare—his own Black Star*! And the trader man was leading out his pony!

For a minute Blue Eagle was stricken dumb. Then

he gave a yell like someone who'd gone crazy and fell against the pony with a thud. But slowly he turned back to all the others, with doubt and caution written on his face. "Why do you bring Black Star again?" he asked them.

The trader, who both laughed and tried to frown, said, "One pony is enough for one piano. Didn't you know the mare is now in foal?"

Gray Wolf and all the others, too, were laughing. "I guess you'll have to keep her now," he said. "Your uncle and I signed an 'owe-you' credit for this plaything your sister longs to have. But both of you are going to help with payments . . ." He couldn't hear the rest his father said for the surge of great commotion that was rising.

Already men were lifting the piano, and all the people came to stare and stand, and to point and poke and look inside and under.

Singing Willow, who by now had got the sheep home and safely in their shelter for the night, also came over to join with the others and see what the excitement was about.

Blue Eagle grinned when suddenly she saw it. Her eyes grew large and lit up like two stars. Then she ran and fell upon the big piano and hugged it just as he had hugged his mare.

Gray Wolf was trying hard to hide his pleasure. "Yes, your brother causes us a lot of woe. He even tried to trade his excellent pony so you could have this toy for idle play."

"His pony! Oh, no—" Quickly she turned to him, her eyes beginning to well up with tears.

But Gray Wolf said sternly, "Now no more wailing.

You've got your piano; he has his mare. And both of you will work to help us buy it. You at the school, he at the trading post."

Then the trader told the girl the plan for payment that he, her uncle, and the mission had made. Everyone had certainly been awfully busy, Blue Eagle thought. She was to teach at school.

"Only part-time; you can still live at home. You'll go there every other week," the trader said. "Your teacher wishes your help with the piano classes. She'll instruct the students those weeks when you're not there. She takes a great deal of pride in your talent for music and thinks you can handle the teaching very well."

Singing Willow seemed delighted with the plan.

"And seeing you so often," the trader added, "your brother won't get homesick while at school."

"*SCHOOL!*" It exploded from Blue Eagle like a bombshell.

"And working for the trader," Gray Wolf said.

"I could use a boy to help me after school hours. There's always lots of work around the store."

"That part, okay," Blue Eagle told the trader. "But not the other part about school."

"The mission thinks it's way past time you started."

"In a pig's eye! I don't plan to start at all."

"School," his father said.

"I can't!"

"*School!*"

"But how *can* I? I'm needed here at home to tend the flock!"

"We'll manage," Gray Wolf said. "Your sister's home now. And all the rest of us can lend a hand." Then he

and the trader left to join the others, for by now the piano had reached the door, and it looked as though there was some sort of trouble.

Blue Eagle spat and kicked a coffee can. No one had even asked him what *he* wanted. They'd been so busy making stupid plans—so busy chopping up this mess of fish tails—they'd just *forgot*! He seethed awhile, then kicked the trailer-truck. But finally he took Black Star by the halter and started toward the shelter with the mare.

At the hogan door he found the sky had fallen. They couldn't get the piano inside. Either the opening was a lot too little or else the piano was much too wide. All the shouts and talking died down to a murmur. On each face was a look of utter doom.

Then Red-Bottle-Stand-Tall said, "This is no problem. Just put the thing in place, then build a room."

"Okay. If mountain won't go to Mohammed, then Mohammed go to mountain," Uncle said, and the big one gave a deep, great roar of laughter that echoed on the mesa with a boom.

Quickly, smiles came back once more to all the faces. And the sky went back up to the sky again as The People fell to making preparations for Singing Willow's special music room.

# CHAPTER XIV

# A Hogan for the Bluebird

SO MANY HANDS ALL WORKING FOR A PURPOSE CAN BUILD a hogan in no time at all. Every day there was an increase in the helpers, for word of Singing Willow's toy had spread.

On the third day, when Blue Eagle came from pasture, the men had almost finished with the roof. But just as he alighted from his pony he saw Red-Bottle-Stand-Tall slip and fall. All the others hurried down and gathered around him, for the tall one had been very badly hurt. This time it seemed his leg was really broken. Someone must go and bring the medicine man.

But at the mention of the great *Hatali*, Red-Bottle-Stand-Tall had a different thought. There wasn't any need to get *Hatali*. Just take him quickly to the hospital. Then he burst into a sudden peal of laughter. He would surely be allowed to enter now. So the men assisted him into a *chidi*, and as they drove the injured one away, he waved back with happy smiles to all the people. At last, the tall one had the entrance pay.

Blue Eagle grinned and turned back to his Black Star to unsaddle her when all at once he saw, from the corner of his eye, a pinto pony and someone standing back against the wall.

Since that night when Johnny fell into disfavor and fled across the desert in disgrace, he had kept himself in hiding from Blue Eagle. Even now young Johnny wouldn't show his face. Standing apart well off from all the others, he was wiggling his toe into the sand. And he looked lonely, as though he felt forsaken.

But Blue Eagle had no anger left by now, for it was almost two moons since the squaw dance. Besides, with Sister well and Black Star back, there was too much *hozoni* for old grudges. He called out *"Ahalani"* to his friend.

As quickly, then, as sun lights up a mountain, the darkness fled from Johnny's full-moon face. With his pinto he came over to Blue Eagle, who had already started toward his friend.

For a moment both boys stood in awkward shyness. Then Blue Eagle said, "I wonder if you've heard that my pony will one day become a mother."

Johnny beamed and said, "I thought, but had not heard."

"Do you think the foal will bear the black star marking?"

"I think it may have markings every place."

Blue Eagle laughed, and Johnny's grin grew wider.

"One half the foal will then belong to you, for your pinto surely is the sire and father."

But the soberness came back to Johnny's face as he said, "My share I give your elder sister, for I was in a hurry at the dance and had to leave before I made the payment. But my half of the new foal will clear the debt."

"It will and more." Blue Eagle spoke with feeling.

Yet all the other words he longed to say seemed quite locked inside. So once again came silence.

Then Blue Eagle said, "I've got a great big woe." He sounded awfully mournful.

"What?" said Johnny.

"School."

"No good."

"I know."

"You going?"

"So they say."

"That's bad."

"I know." He shrugged.

"But then," said Johnny, "it may be that I'll give it one more try."

Suddenly both grinned as though they plotted something; then began to laugh. They laughed till they held their sides.

But finally Johnny climbed back onto his pinto, and as he turned the pony's head about, Blue Eagle told his friend to go in beauty. And in pride and beauty Johnny rode away.

While the boys had talked, twilight had crept around them. Klenhanoi, the moon goddess, now arose. Blue Eagle watched her blanket all the desert. She lights the way for Johnny to go home, he thought. Then from the music hogan came a magic that sprinkled gold upon the silver night. So the sheepherder reached up for Black Star's halter and went over by the door to stand outside.

In the hogan they had built for the piano, his grandmother was putting things in place. Already she had blessed the house with pollen, and there was a new contentment in her face. Her head was even nodding to the rhythm of Sister's music, marking out the time.

Then the music stopped, and Sister's voice was saying, "Grandmother, would you stay with me tonight? Let us sleep in here beside the new piano." Pleased, the Old One made the sign of her consent. But as she started over to the opening with the wooden door, his sister spoke again. "Do you not feel the blanket is less clumsy? I think it gives so much more beauty, too."

Then the music magic started up again, and the bluebird in the tree sang out an answer.

When the Old One came to hang the woolen blanket, Blue Eagle saw the look upon her face. But the blanket fell to shut him from that splendor—so he turned back to the wonder of the night.

In beauty it was finished.